Though None Go With Me

Lorene Masters

Master Moments Books

For more information: lorenemasters@gmail.com

First paperback edition April 2026

ISBN: 978-1-7373861-7-9

Contents

Introduction

Though none go with me on the narrow way, still I will follow.

Easier said than done, especially when you're completely abandoned, and it feels minimal to whisper those words surrounded by love and acceptance. And due to abundant blessings, the Lord feels close. *Yes, I will go on alone* is easy to say when spoken in peace, rooted in confidence, having never known long-lasting loneliness, nor expecting an existence without human comfort. It's simple to believe your faith will carry you through trials when your days are filled with a loving family, good friends, food, shelter, and hope for tomorrow. But reality shifts drastically when loved ones betray and forsake you, friends disappear, and you're stranded in a world entirely lacking human love. Despair then becomes overwhelming, pain turning into a relentless, unwelcome shadow. Your heart hardens and cracks like a desert that has not seen rain for many seasons. Only God truly understands the depth of your suffering when you're lost in this barren wilderness.

What is the narrow way, and why did Jesus tell us to take this solitary road less traveled? The phrase "narrow way" is an important biblical metaphor found in the Sermon on the Mount in the Gospel of Matthew. Jesus clearly contrasts two paths in life, each leading to a very different destination. "Enter by the narrow gate. For the gate is wide and the way is easy that leads to destruction, and those who enter by it are many. For the gate is narrow and the way is hard that leads to life, and those who find it are few." (Matthew 7:13,14)

Choosing the narrow way isn't just a gentle suggestion but a crucial, life-changing decision. It features a "narrow gate" that leads to eternal life. It requires true, sacrificial love from the heart—deep roots, complete openness, and the surrender of your entire self to God. Walking this path requires a deep commitment: living according to God's wisdom and carefully obeying and imitating Jesus' teachings, with a transformed life evident.

The wide gate and broad paths are filled with fun-loving people and great pleasure, and can seem right, but in truth, they are dangerous and lead to destruction. And beware, for often, a life of outward righteousness hides inner corruption—an illusion of faith. This broad way is tempting, heavily traveled, and appears popular, but it ends in eternal ruin. It offers a false sense of temporary comfort, acceptance, belonging, and pleasure, yet ultimately leads to hell.

The narrow way involves more than just outward actions; it requires a complete transformation of the heart, filled with deep love and a strong desire to follow Jesus—the only true path to salvation and eternal life. It emphasizes self-denial, sacrifice, and a constant willingness to endure loneliness, face hardships, and take on challenges. The narrow path is illuminated by God's Holy Word—your constant guide in darkness. This journey calls for dying to self-centeredness and living fully for Jesus, seeking only to please your Master while He is away, and being ready to receive approval and eternal life when He returns. and declares, "Well done, thou good and faithful servant." (Matthew 25:21 KJV)

Choose your path carefully—every moment counts, and the stakes are incredibly high. Your salvation depends on this decision. It's a journey of building character, and you must commit to walking it daily, even if no one else joins you. And soon you may realize that you will arrive at the gates of your eternal home all alone, for no one was able to go with you. But do not despair, for you will be greeted by a multitude of souls and angels waiting for your arrival with great joy. Your father will kiss you and welcome you home forever, and your joy will never end.

01

The Call

"For a long time, you have been hidden in the shadows by those who cannot see your beauty and calling. But you were always found and known by Jesus. Now you have the choice to step out of the shadows of uncertainty and follow in His footsteps, even though the path is difficult and lonely. How does one follow Him into life on the narrow way, you wonder? The path can be hard to find and sometimes seems impossible, but it can be discovered when you look in the right place. In the darkness, His word will light your way. By forsaking the world as you seek to follow, even if no one else goes with you, you will live forevermore."

"How do you know this, George?" Faustina asked, incredulously.

"I have been there many times. The path is well known to those who travel it often."

"How can this be? You are younger than me. When did you find this hidden path?"

George grew quiet. He smiled and sat on a smooth rock beside a well-worn trail that led to the cave where I would meet John and Daniel. I hoped the path he mentioned was nearby, the place where I would meet my Lord.

"I am older than you realize, and I know more than I have told you."

"Who are you, really?"

"I am George, your guide into an eternal world where time stands still," he said, bowing slightly, his smile warm enough to melt your heart, for he was quite beautiful.

"I have been there many times without your help. Why do I need you now?"

"Jesus knows and sees the path ahead, the dangers, the fears, and even the joys and pleasures. You trust Him?"

"Of course."

"So trust me, for I receive my direction from Him."

"Alright. He has told me to go to the cave and meet with John and Daniel."

"THE John and Daniel?" he asked, genuinely surprised, for not many were privileged to meet two of the greatest men of the Bible.

"Yes. I know John well, but I only know Daniel from what I have read."

"Have they met each other?"

"Well, since they are both in eternity now, I assume they have."

"Interesting. They both spoke of the end of the world. I imagine they are good friends. Do you know the way?"

"I did, unless it has become overgrown."

"You face more than an overgrown path—many roads vie for your choice, yet only one leads to true life. This is a crucial test, designed to guide you onto the path to eternal life and keep you there. As the end of time draws near, you'll witness and understand the fierce struggle facing the entire world. Many will be deceived into believing that all roads lead home, but you'll see through the lie. Prepare to experience sights and feelings that will shake your very soul. Yet remember: no trial is ever wasted, and your reward will be immense when the books are opened. On that incredible day, you'll proclaim that nothing compares to the glory soon to be revealed in you. Your joy will be boundless, everlasting!

"Good! I see you did not bring any food, only water. That is all you will need for now. Food would weigh you down. For now, your sustenance is doing His will. Please know that you will not always see me, but I will be there when you need to talk. Even when I am not present, you will be aware of me and feel my prayers for you. I pray not only for you but for all of humankind in the valley of decision."

"I truly believe I am ready, for at this moment, I have no other option but to follow the path He has chosen for me. So with all my heart, let's begin. And from the bottom of my heart, thank you, George, for saying yes to Jesus and helping guide me on this journey of a lifetime."

02

Getting There

What had once seemed an ancient trail to the cave was now tangled with thick weeds and sharp rocks, leaving Sister Faustina unsure whether she was on the right path. The uncertainty gnawed at her, made worse by the fact that she had never dared to walk this way alone so late in the season. Leaves, now tinged with autumn hues, signaled the approach of winter. A pungent smell lingered in the air, as if the tired green trees knew it was time to lose their color. Just yesterday, a message had come urging her to hurry to the Cave of Satar. Its mysterious instructions for the next part of her journey had kept her awake all night in prayer. Her life, named after Sister Faustina of Poland, had been a constant effort to honor that saintly legacy, expressing her devotion even in the smallest acts. Called "Sista" by her younger brother Nathan when he was learning to talk, she treasured the nickname, her heart swelling with pride every time she heard it.

In this moment of uncertainty and growing awareness of her responsibilities, she felt a quiet connection to her namesake's legacy, ready to face whatever challenges lay ahead. How had she received the message to go? She might say it came on the breeze that cooled her brow after a long day in the garden, or that someone whispered it to her as she headed to the market to sell her fruit. But it was not so dramatic. She simply knew she had to go.

It was time to visit her friends, those God had blessed her with. Friends no one else could see, though George claimed he saw them when she spoke of them. He could see into the unseen world, so it seemed natural that he, too, had eyes to perceive what others could not. No one else knew of the visions that grew more frequent each year. Not even her husband. He was often drunk, and even if he had noticed, he would not have cared. He wanted nothing to do with such things.

Letting go of what lay behind her and reaching for what lay ahead was not easy. She felt lonely, with few companions, and knew that once she entered the cave, there would be no one beside her except her heavenly visitors. The thought of that coming absence settled deep within her, a quiet, heavy loneliness.

Again, her Lord called, and the only way to quiet the stirring in her soul was to obey.

"Come to the garden alone and leave the passions of this world behind," He told her. "Forsake all, and I will fill you. Hunger for Me alone, and you will know the peace and joy that would otherwise elude you."

"Another fast, Faustina?" her estranged family asked. "Who is telling you to do this? Phantoms again, whispering to you in the night?"

"Oh dear, she will be telling me she saw me in Hell again," her husband said with a laugh, mocking her, his tongue out and eyes wide in jest.

She paid no attention to their questions or their ridicule. She trusted that she had heard His voice. Had not the fruit of her previous fasts made that clear? The change in her heart, the quiet purity of her motives, the renewed love she felt for others. Even her body had responded. Old aches had faded, headaches had lessened, and her strength had returned.

Her Lord never forced her. She was always free to choose.

Still, the thought of the hunger to come sent a hollow ache through her, a kind of emptiness that reached beyond her body. She had endured it before, both the physical hunger and the deeper ache within her soul, yet each time it returned, it tested her again. The enemy of her soul whispered against the call, urging her to remain, to eat, to live as she once had, where others feasted on life and all its pleasures without question.

She knew her hunger was more than physical. When the call came, she had tried to silence it with food, but it never worked. The fresh bread she baked, spread with butter and sweet strawberry jelly, turned bitter in her stomach as the Lord's quiet urging persisted. She knew better than to resist it now.

Her Lord was patient. He told her she could come whenever she was ready. Everything had been prepared. John and Daniel were already waiting.

Why were the body's desires so hard to resist? The same ancient pull, the same quiet temptation that had followed humanity since the beginning. The urge to turn away, to choose another path, to satisfy the self rather than surrender it.

And now she felt it again.

Feeling suddenly weak, Faustina paused to rest. She sat beside George and, before she knew it, drifted into sleep on the soft grass near the rock where he sat.

And then she was dreaming.

The knocking came first, low and distant, then louder, more insistent. The Lord's voice followed, calling to her, echoing through her soul. Her room seemed to come alive, filled with the presence of those who had once walked the Earth but now belonged to another realm. Yet they were here, vivid and unmistakable.

Their presence surrounded her, pressing gently against her senses, awakening something deeper within her. Then another figure appeared, one she did not recognize. She did not know his name or why he had come, but she felt no fear. Guided by the Lord, she asked to go further.

Everything around her began to move, shifting and alive. Each day she had sought the Lord through fasting and prayer, and now He was revealing more to her, scenes unfolding before her eyes with a clarity she could not ignore. More figures appeared, each carrying a weight she could not yet understand.

Ezekiel. Jeremiah. John the Revelator. Isaiah.

And then Daniel.

They stood among her, real and present. She tried to take it in, but it was too much at once. Too much to understand, too much to carry. A deep exhaustion settled over her as she struggled to endure what was being shown.

And just as suddenly as it began, it was gone.

"Oh Lord, lead me there. Guide me along the path to the beauty of Your garden, where the scent of flowers reflects Your beauty, You whom I love with all my heart. Free me from fear of hunger, lack, and loneliness. Uphold me when the enemy's voice reminds me that I am alone on this journey. Teach me not to fear the emptiness that comes with fasting, knowing that as You have promised, if I empty myself, I will be filled with You. There is so much You wish to show me. I want to see even the hidden things in darkness, trusting that Your light will guide me through every shadow."

03

John and Daniel

The weather was like a feral cat, sometimes gentle, sometimes startled and fleeing for cover. John and Daniel, warm and dry inside the cave, waited patiently. They knew a call had gone out for an end-time prophet, someone willing to fast and wait, faithfully recording all that was revealed.

They understood how the Lord's revelations came. At times, visions arrived quickly. At other times, they unfolded slowly. There were long stretches of waiting, moments filled with nothing but silence and the command to remain still. Sometimes the meaning of what was seen became clearer over time. Other times, it faded, sealed by the Lord for another season, another place.

The prophet walked a difficult and lonely path, even when others stood nearby. Still, they continued, holding to the promise of a glorious garden waiting at the end. A garden of love, where every longing would finally be fulfilled.

John and Daniel had served faithfully on Earth, and now they lived in eternity, where time no longer held sway. They could see what was happening below and were permitted to interact with those their Lord had chosen. Today, their minds were full, yet all worry had left them, for worry belonged to those still bound to Earthly bodies.

John spoke with quiet certainty. "She will come, Daniel. I know her."

"I believe you, John. Let us speak, then. Let us reflect on what has already been prophesied and fulfilled, rather than on what still lies ahead for the Earth. The Lord told me to seal up the vision, for it was for many days yet to come. You struggled to understand what I saw, did you not? I did as well. It left me exhausted. I lay ill for days, unable to make sense of it. Tell me again, John. Tell me what you saw. I cannot rest until I hear it from you, even though, deep within me, I know it will be just as you witnessed."

"Prophets know these things, do they not, Daniel?"

"Yes. And still, all prophets must wait for their fulfillment. They must remain faithful and trust in what they do not yet understand. The flesh is weak, as the Messiah said. It resists the waiting."

"That is true. Yet He draws near and reassures all who hunger to know the truth. And how that nearness deepens when one fasts, when He calls the faithful away into greater intimacy, revealing things they could not have known."

"So, what do you know about the one who is coming, John?"

"Her name is Faustina. She has endured a great deal. She never knew her father and was raised by her mother, who led a troubled life. Although her mother remained married, there was infidelity. Faustina grew up with many siblings, but she was never fully accepted. She has experienced profound loneliness since childhood.

"She married young and needed care when she fell ill with a rare blood condition that left her weak and exhausted. Her husband, Manly, is harsh in spirit and often drinks. Although he can keep his job, he mocks her faith and encourages others to do the same.

"She has two daughters, Sara and Grace, whom she loves deeply, yet they remain distant from her. They have built their lives elsewhere, and their husbands are unwilling to welcome her. They see her faith as excessive and narrow. They have chosen to keep their distance, and she feels it. It is as if she has been forgotten.

"But she is not without help. George has been her companion and support in ways she doesn't fully understand. Yet, he will also cause trouble for her, as you will see."

"George? I know George."

"You do? Then keep what you know to yourself. Faustina doesn't yet understand who he is. Or why he is in her life. He has only told her that he is older than he appears," John continued.

"She has a faithful, tender soul. Yet because of all she has endured, she struggles to see her worth. Her beauty is not outward but within; it is eternal. She follows God's voice and encourages others to do the same. Still, she often feels she's not doing enough. A heaviness lingers in her, a quiet sorrow.

"I have seen her before, on the Island of Patmos, when the Lord brought her there. She was shown glimpses of eternity, though in a simpler way than I was."

Daniel let out a soft laugh. "Any vision would be simpler than yours, John. I am still trying to understand it all. Like an eagle? Could you not have simply said airplane?"

"No one knew of airplanes then," John replied with a smile. "And what about you? Did you understand the ram and the goat, or the great statue? We see them clearly now."

"Yes, we do. But that is a conversation for another time."

"It is a joy to see clearly now, in these eternal bodies."

"Yes. As for Faustina, she often doubts herself. She questions why Jesus would choose her —someone unknown, someone she believes is insignificant. She thinks there must be others, more qualified, more visible and established—someone whose words would reach many.

"She does not yet realize that what she writes is meant for a specific time. Most of her writings go unseen because the Lord has instructed her not to promote herself. She views her words as a way to encourage others, yet that door remains shut for now.

"She is called to seek Him, to write what He reveals, to withdraw into quiet places. To step away from family, from comfort, even from food at times, so she can hear Him clearly. This path is not easy for her.

"She looks at those in the world who write, who publish, who are seen and celebrated, and compares herself to them and feels small. But that is not her calling. She is being shaped for something different.

"He has spoken to her about this. He has told her, 'Do you know what doors I will open tomorrow? Why be discouraged? I could do these things in a moment, but there is purpose in the waiting. I am laying a foundation. When I bring you forward, you will have something true to say. You will speak for Me, not for yourself. I will guide you. Be faithful. Do not be troubled by what others think of what I have given you.'"

"Remember, she is still in the body and will only visit us as much as she can stand, as much as the Lord permits. So behave your best, Daniel."

Daniel smiled. "I always am. I cannot say the same for you."

"She knows me," John said gently. "I think of her as my sister."

"When is she going to arrive?"

"Soon. George is already where he needs to be, helping her find the way."

04

His Way is Perfect

"For your Maker is your husband, the Lord of hosts is His name." (Isaiah 54:5 ESV)

Faustina was excited to find this verse during her early-morning reading. Having married young and unhappily, she often turned to the Lord for comfort, viewing Him as her husband. Her husband, Manly, was often at the town's bars, drinking and dancing with any woman willing. The first time she saw him with another woman, it broke something inside her.

"You are too good for me," he murmured one night, stumbling home drunk, his voice heavy and unsteady. The bar had been empty of women willing to go with him, leaving him restless and bitter. Then, without warning, regret washed over him. Tears filled his eyes as he spoke.

"Your heart is too pure," he said, his voice soft now, almost pleading. "I just want to have fun. I want to party, to live freely. You won't even sit with me and share a drink sometimes. Honestly, I don't see us lasting. You should find a man who goes to church and lives the way you do."

In the quiet darkness of those nights, Faustina often considered leaving him, but she had nowhere to go. She clung to a fragile hope that he might change, though it flickered weakly, like a dying flame. It felt distant, almost impossible. His father was a deacon. His mother dedicated herself to charity, a life that seemed so far removed from the man he had become. The gap between what could have been and what was grew wider with each passing day, pushing her deeper into a quiet sorrow.

There were moments when he tried. At times, he agreed to attend prayer meetings with a friend who had chosen to stop drinking. But it never lasted. Without alcohol, he was still restless and unsettled. He constantly demanded her attention, asking questions he never waited for answers to, pressing her to explain things he had no desire to understand. Faustina felt the weight of it. There was no way to reach him.

But she remained faithful. And continued forward, trusting the Lord to deal with Manly in His time.

What a fool I was.

The thought rose within her without warning.

Were men truly sent to break hearts, as her mother Irena had often said?

Irena was a woman of captivating charm and fleeting affections. She loved deeply but never for long. Still, she always made one thing clear: none of her children were a mistake. Even when Faustina struggled to believe it, she knew her mother meant it.

Her mother's lovers had always been handsome, almost unreal in their beauty. Faustina remembered the quiet nights, the sound of her mother crying at the kitchen table, whispering to herself through heartbreak after another man had left her for someone else. The soft clink of glass, the silence that followed, the weight of something breaking again.

Irena didn't drink often, but when she did, it was impossible not to notice. The bottle left behind the next morning told the whole story. Faustina would pour it out in silence, making a quiet promise to herself that she would never turn to that kind of escape.

Despite everything, she believed her mother was good. Broken in places, yes, but still full of love for her children, holding them together as best she could.

To protect herself from loneliness, Irena kept people close. There was always someone she could call when the nights felt overwhelming. Not all the children knew who their fathers were. As they grew older, some began to guess, piecing together clues from fragments and similarities. Even Irena did not always know the full truth.

It had once troubled Faustina deeply that she would never know her own father. But that ache had softened over time. She had fully given her heart to the Lord, seeing in Him both Father and Husband, now and forever. She had chosen to remain faithful to Him.

And yet, there were moments when loneliness crept back in. She yearned for someone to talk to, someone who could understand the things she was seeing. Someone present, someone genuine, someone who could walk beside her. Not to replace what she had with the Lord, but to share the burden and joy of it.

Still, she reminded herself that she belonged to Jesus. She was His bride. So, she held tightly to Him as the visions grew stronger and her life pulled her further into solitude, away from everything she once knew.

Every day, she prayed for guidance. Just the day before, He had told her it was time to find John and Daniel in the cave.

She was thankful for George. He worked long hours in the fields, but he was always there when she needed him. That morning, they met along the path that led toward the river and the hidden caves of Mount Sirat.

She had just woken from a springtime dream. The ground was soft under her feet, and flowers blooming along the mountain trail. Lilies, lilacs, roses. Their scent filled the air. She inhaled deeply, thinking, This must be what Heaven feels like.

She had reached out to pick a lilac to place in her hair.

And then she woke.

Her bag was already packed. When she looked outside, autumn had fully arrived. The air was cool, the sky overcast, with gold leaves carried by the wind. She stepped onto the path and soon saw George approaching, smiling as if he already knew.

"What are you doing out here? Let me guess. The Voice told you to come?"

"Yes. But if you're going to mock me, I won't tell you anything more. It's enough that my family laughs at me when I pray and talk about Jesus.

"Pay them no mind," he said. "They do not understand what they cannot see. If it cannot be touched, it must not be real. Is that not what your husband says?"

"How did you know that was what troubled me? They say I think I am better than them because I go to church so often."

"I know that is not true. Now tell me, what did the Voice say?"

"I am to go to the cave and meet John and Daniel."

He paused. "Then we need to be careful who we tell. They may not understand. They might try to stop you."

"Do you believe me?"

"Yes. I have been listening as well, and I was told you would come this way. So I believe you are hearing from God."

They shared a quiet understanding. For a moment, she experienced what it felt like to be truly seen.

"I must warn you," George said softly. "There is darkness along the way to Mount Sirat. Not everything that appears good is good. There are those who deceive."

"Oh... can we pray? I feel uneasy. And suddenly, I am so tired. I do not know if I can keep going."

The moment they joined hands, a weakness came over her, and she sank to the ground as the vision began.

The cave lay ahead of her, illuminated with light. Daniel was inside. John stood next to him. They led her further inside. She felt no fear—only light, brighter than anything she had ever seen.

Five great tables stood inside the cave, resembling large drafting tables, covered with images and designs of what was to come. The end would unfold just as the Scriptures had said. But within those words were countless lives, many choices, each carrying eternal weight. The valley of decision stretched before many. Too many were choosing darkness, drawn toward deception, toward allegiance with what opposed the Lord.

She found herself sitting at a table, a pencil in her hand. She didn't know what to do.

She had never intended to create this way, but something inside her changed. It was as if she had been ready for this without realizing it.

Jesus was there.

He spoke to her gently, calling her to become a vessel, just as He had called John and Daniel. She must be emptied of herself. There could be no desire for recognition, no pursuit of success. Everything must belong to Him. His glory alone would fill her, becoming both her hunger and her satisfaction.

She would be misunderstood and hurt. Those closest to her would turn away, pushing her further into quiet obscurity. There would be moments when it felt like a loss.

But it was not punishment.

It was space.

Space to hear. Space to see. Space to become what she had been called to be.

There would come a time when nothing else would matter. No one else would matter.

Only Jesus.

And she had not realized how much it would cost her to reach that place.

05

The Cave at Sirat Mountain

Thus, Sister Faustina set out to meet John and Daniel. George gave her clear directions on how to get there and told her to memorize them before discarding the map, in case she was captured.

"Captured?" she exclaimed. "By whom?"

"There is danger along the way. Once you arrive, you will be safe, but the journey will test you greatly."

Sister Faustina, thankful for the map now stored in her memory, started her walk with a sense of lightness, though her soul carried quiet worries. She was happy to follow the Voice, knowing there was no place she would rather be than on the path her Lord had chosen for her.

The ground around the meeting rock and along the trail was rough, uneven, and strewn with stones. It pressed painfully against her feet, even though her best shoes. The air was fresh, yet beneath it lingered something dark and foul. Strange sounds, like distant animal cries, echoed from both near and far, making her tremble. The weather shifted suddenly. Dark clouds gathered where sunlight had been moments before, then just as quickly dispersed. She knew she had to walk these places alone, with only the Lord beside her. Still, there were moments she wished someone could walk with her on the journeys He called her to.

He often spoke to her: "Obey my Voice quickly and do not fear the danger. All will be well if you know you are doing My will."

Though none go with me, I will still follow!

As soon as those words formed in her mind, two grotesque baboons appeared before her. One was more revolting than the other. The larger one chased the smaller, which had blood streaming from its ear. They seemed unaware of her presence, yet she stood frozen, unable to move.

She wanted to help.

Why was the stronger one hurting the weaker?

Before she could understand what was happening, more pairs appeared, surrounding her and closing her in. The smaller ones, which she thought were females, had blood pouring from their heads. The larger ones kept striking and biting them repeatedly. The females' screams filled the air, growing louder and louder. Faustina dropped to the ground, covering her ears, but the sounds continued without stopping.

"Jesus..."

Her voice trembled as she cried out.

Suddenly, angels appeared. They fought the baboons until the females broke free and ran into the mountains. Then the chaos ended just as quickly as it had started.

Faustina remained still. Slowly, she opened her eyes.

Everything was quiet.

There was no blood on the ground.

What just happened? Did I dream this? I am too afraid to move.

"Jesus! Please help me!"

At that moment, George dropped down on a thick rope from one of the tall, dark trees above her.

"George! How did you get there? Did you see what just happened?"

He looked at her calmly. "What you saw is not merely of nature. It reflects the hearts of men. There are those who harm, who dominate, who treat women as if they have no worth. This will increase. Those who follow darkness will justify such acts. They will silence cries for help. They will enslave and degrade, believing they have the right."

Faustina's breath caught.

"The only true freedom is found in Jesus," he continued. "In Him, women live with dignity, strength, and love, reflecting His image. But those who harm others and reject what is good will face the consequences of their choices. They will stand alone in what they have chosen."

"But George... why did I have to see this? What does the Lord want me to do with this?"

"This is why you need to meet with John and Daniel. They will show you the battle the Lord is calling you to fight, what to pray for, and how to stay on the right path."

"I cannot forget what I saw," she whispered. "I will never forget that poor female baboon."

"You are not meant to forget. What you have seen will inspire you to seek truth and to share the love you know in Jesus. He is not revealing these things to torment you but to guide you into intercession for the lost. And what is suffered here is small compared to the horror of an endless hell."

"Yes," she said softly. "Thank you for reminding me. I forget sometimes that I am not here simply to be content. I have been called to seek and to save the lost."

"With each battle you face, the Lord is preparing you. You must learn to stand. Be equipped with the armor of God."

Suddenly, she was alone again.

George disappears so often.

The path ahead of her narrowed, and darkness settled in. Faustina took a sip of water and prepared to move forward.

Yea though I walk through the valley of the shadow of death I will fear no evil for......(Psalm 23:4 KJV)

It felt like she had been walking for hours. Darkness surrounded her, broken only by faint glimpses of light. Her lantern flickered, barely holding against the shadows. The trees and rocks seemed to shift, forming shapes that unsettled her. Eerie sounds echoed around her, whispering her name.

A choking smell filled the air, making her feel sick. Suddenly, it disappeared, replaced by the sweet scent of roses. The sudden change unsettled her even more.

She forced herself to focus on the narrow path ahead, where Jesus was.

She steadied her breathing, refusing to give in to fear. If the Lord had called her here, He would protect her and see her through. She would fulfill the purpose set before her.

Oh, Lord... please let it be so. I feel so fragile, so worn. But I know You are with me. Even when I cannot feel it.

At last, she saw it.

The entrance to the cave.

Partially hidden by trees yet glowing faintly from within. A fire had been kept burning for her.

"Hello..."

Her voice echoed into the cave.

"Come in, my child! Come in. We have been expecting you. It is safe here. There is danger outside, but you need not fear, for He has prepared a table for you."

"John! Hello! I missed you!"

She ran to him, tears spilling freely, the weight of the journey and the relief of arriving overtaking her.

"And I you," he said gently. "Though it feels as though no time has passed."

"To me, it feels like years since we last spoke."

"Ah, yes. That is the way of the body. I have been wanting to go over some thoughts I had with you about...", John began.

"Not now, John," Daniel said with a smile. "He has been rehearsing everything he wanted to tell you since you last spoke."

"What is this place?" Faustina asked, looking around at the well-lit space and the chairs set for comfort. "It feels different from other caves."

"It is a place of safety for you," Daniel said. "Sit, and we will tell you what awaits you. Or as much as you can bear right now."

After a soothing cup of tea and warm blueberry scones, they began.

"Remember, Sister Faustina, when Jesus said that the way to life is narrow?"

"John, she was not there," Daniel said.

"Yes. Then, do you remember when you read about the narrow way?"

"The Bible? Yes, I do."

"There is a broad road that leads to destruction, and a narrow path that leads to life. The path you are on now is the way. He is that way. The only way that leads to eternal life."

Faustina nodded.

"The Lord will reveal to you the many paths people will take. These paths may seem right but lead to death. You will see them. You will experience them. And you will write the details down so others can read and hopefully turn before it's too late. This mountain is called Sirat. Some believe it's a bridge to paradise, but that's not true. Only through Jesus is there life. He is the gate. All other gates lead to death."

"Will I experience each path? Or only observe them?"

"Both."

She hesitated. "Will it be difficult? Will I suffer?"

"Yes. It will be difficult. You will suffer. But you will not be alone. There will be temptation. Some paths will seem appealing. But you must stand in the truth. Ask Him to show you where each path leads and how to turn away from it. Many believe they are on the right path, but if it is not through Jesus Christ, the Son of God, who came in the flesh, died, and rose again, it leads to death."

"How can I withstand this, John?" I lamented.

Suddenly, I was in the spirit realm, surrounded by demons of different levels and ranks. Confusion overtook me, but then Jesus spoke.

I am not fighting battles alone. I am solely responsible for my current position, for this moment, and for the battles He has called me to face until victory is achieved.

By the power of the Holy Spirit, I stood and fought. One by one, the demons vanished. Beyond them, I saw more. Legions surrounded leaders, those who shaped nations and prepared the way for the gospel or the rejection of it. I realized I was only witnessing this for a moment. Soon, the door would close.

"Today is the day of salvation, for tomorrow you may meet God and be called to account for your life. Know Jesus now! Tomorrow might be too late. There will be no applause if you choose the way of Satan. Alone for eternity, you will face torment, pain, and vivid memories, with no second chances to choose the path of life.

"I will go, Lord, and remain faithful to You and to the calling You gave me. Though the way be narrow, lonely, and hard, I will go. I will be faithful in this hour."

"Very good, my child," John said. "You are ready to walk the paths mankind will choose. And through what you will share, many will turn while there is time. The night is coming quickly."

06

The Path of False Religion

"Although many false religions exist, one will become dominant, and the Antichrist will emerge from it. This so-called religion is more than a heretical belief; it is a political ideology designed to conquer the world," John said the next morning as they sat around the table.

The pomegranate tea was excellent. Faustina remarked that its flavor was beyond anything she had tasted before. As they discussed the roads ahead of her journey, a white, smoky presence appeared in the adjacent room where the drafting tables stood, just as the Lord had shown Faustina before her arrival. They immediately rose and moved toward it.

They stood in silence as a woman dressed entirely in black appeared on paper at the first drafting table, her body covered from head to toe. The air smelled of old paper and ink, as if what was being revealed had always existed and was only now coming into view. When Faustina looked more closely, she saw that only the woman's eyes were visible. There was sadness in them, as if she were trapped and had already accepted her condition.

The figure moved slowly, yet with a quiet certainty.

Then she began to grow.

Her black garment spread outward like a vast cover. Inside it, women appeared who had never taken faith seriously but were now drawn into this false religion, believing it to be good and loving. They brought their daughters and other young girls. They giggled softly, as if playing a game, unaware of what was unfolding.

The mothers, their hearts heavy with no easy alternative, willingly gave up their children, convinced they were doing what was right and pleasing to God.

No one was searching for them.

Soon, they will not be found.

Then the wider call began. Its sound was demonic and seductive, making you want to cover your ears yet also give in to the pull to come.

Others saw what was opening, as though a veil had been lifted. A voice spread outward, persuasive and sweet, calling to those who would listen.

"Hurry. Hurry. Now is the time. Come. All who long for something more. Come and receive what you have been missing."

The second image appeared as mysterious as the first.

The woman spoke again, her voice now full of promise. She described a world that felt whole, complete, and welcoming—a place of comfort, provision, and belonging. A world where everything was accessible, everyone was included, and no one would be left out.

At the edge of this vision, Faustina saw others stepping forward.

Some who called themselves Christians.

Some were drawn by what seemed like love. Others had no firm foundation and saw no danger in it. They reasoned that all belief must lead to the same end, believing there couldn't be harm in something that appeared so welcoming.

Others came because of resentment.

They carried memories of cruelty, rules enforced without understanding, and pain tied to what they had once been taught. Their anger had grown, even though they could no longer clearly identify its source. It had taken hold within them, shaped by wounds they had never shown to others.

The cry rose from them.

Hate. Hate. Hate.

And yet, even in their voices, there was confusion.

They did not fully understand what they were rejecting. Only that they no longer wanted it.

The deception deepened.

Faustina observed those who had once known the Lord. Children raised in truth, now turning away, attracted by something that seemed easier, softer, and more accepting. Their eyes were empty, their steps unsure, yet they pressed on.

She could not bear it.

"Jesus... what can be done?"

He was there.

He had always been there.

"Pray, my child. Each soul must choose Me for themselves. They must release what was done wrongly in My name. They must forgive what they have seen in others. I am not the harm they have known. I am not the failure of men. I am the truth that leads to forgiveness and eternal life."

His voice remained steady.

"I heal those who come to Me. I restore what has been broken. But no one can deny Me and claim they did not know. Every soul is aware of Me. That awareness will either grow or it will fade. There is no stillness in it."

Faustina listened, trembling.

"Religion is what a person chooses to place above all else. Even those who claim to believe in nothing have placed their own understanding there. This is not freedom. It is deception. When a person places himself above truth, he creates a false god in his own image.

"Choose now. Life is brief. No one knows when their life will be required. Do not delay."

The weight of His words settled deeply.

As she reflected on what He had said, the woman in black continued to expand, reaching beyond what Faustina could fully grasp. It was no longer just one path. It was many, spreading rapidly, drawing more into itself.

"Faustina, do not be afraid of what you see. You are being shown these things so you will pray. And as you pray, the burden will lift. There are those who will answer the call. There are those who will carry the truth. But much of what you are called to do will require waiting. Not everything unfolds at once. I am merciful, and I desire that none would be lost."

Faustina felt something shift within her.

"I did not understand before... but I do now."

John stepped closer.

"You don't need to rush to share everything you are shown," he said gently. "Some things you will speak. Some things you will carry. The One who gives the word will also carry it where it must go. That is not your burden. Yours is to listen, to obey, and to be ready."

He studied her quietly, as though he could see through every unspoken thought.

"He knows what you carry," John continued. "You are not alone in that. Many have walked this path before you."

Faustina lowered her eyes.

"It does not disqualify you," he said. "Pain does not remove you from His purpose. You will not reach a place in this life where you no longer feel it. Some things must be accepted. And in that place, you learn to seek His comfort and to see beyond what you feel."

His voice softened.

"There is joy in His presence. Not in what comes from it. Not in what it produces. But in Him. You know this. And there is more still to be found."

Faustina felt the truth of that settle in her.

"You have been called into His presence," John said. "Not because you are perfect, but because you are willing. He knows your failures. He knows your weakness. And still, He has chosen you."

Tears filled her eyes.

"Thank you, John..."

She lifted her voice.

"O Jesus, call the faithful to pray for the children of this generation, those who are being drawn away by what they do not understand."

07

Woman in White

The woman, once dressed in black, now appears cloaked in a haunting white. Yet this white is merely a disguise, a thin layer masking decay beneath, like rotten wood coated with fresh paint. Many do not see what lies beneath. They are deceived by the darkness hidden behind the false front. She greets everyone with an enchanting smile and a warm embrace, enticing them with promises of lavish food, camaraderie, and a false sense of security and belonging.

"All are welcome," she cries, sweeping her arm toward family-friendly activities, games, conversation, and books. It feels like being pulled into a wind tunnel as she draws the crowds toward her, presenting treasures on the other side as wonderful and safe, the place to be. But soon the door will close on this great illusion, and all who enter will be trapped. The woman quickly turns, and suddenly she is clothed in black again, while her captives wear chains. Families are torn apart. Women are covered from head to toe in black because their beauty stirs demonic lust in men. Children are taken from their families and handed over to men to do with as they wish. Food and life are cut off if anyone refuses to conform. Love brought them in, but hatred now holds them captive as Satan's final plans unfold and are embraced by the ignorant and lost. Many who have long sounded the alarm are silenced. Soon, even their lives will be taken if they try to escape their bondage.

The woman keeps twirling, shifting between black and white, confusing the world. False prophets emerge, and she bows to them. False signs in the sky prompt her to worship false gods descending from above. Deception is at an all-time high, yet few are alarmed. People remain asleep, sedated by the false, enticing oil from Satan, who pretends to be the coming Messiah they have all waited for. However, the faithful saints of the Lord carry extra oil of the Holy Spirit as they await the true Messiah, and they are not fooled. Those who have brought only a little oil are left in darkness as their lamps dim and darkness fills them. They stumble like drunk men in broad daylight. But they do not care.

The woman in black's seductive style inspires more people to wear black. They walk in darkness yet believe it is light. They worship Satan as an angel of light and fail to see him for who he truly is. They hate the true children of God and try to kill them. Some are physically harmed, but their souls are forever safe and alive in Jesus. They do not fear darkness, for they know that Jesus, the Son of God who came in the flesh, has walked this path before. New courage is poured out upon the faithful.

Many are wise and refuse to be seduced by the woman in black. They, too, swirl and dance, but with the oil of the Lord within them. They move gracefully, clothed in beautiful white garments, attentive to the voice of their Master, who now speaks even more loudly in their souls as darkness falls over the world. They must recognize His voice now, for vision is clouding as Satan makes his final stand. Many who did not heed the Lord's voice in brighter days now find themselves confused, without a compass to guide them. Yet many who suffer for the Lord are happy, wearing the garment of praise, because they will be purified and made white. The true children of the Lord frustrate the followers of darkness.

The woman in black has grown quite large, now filling the entire third canvas. An unseen hand has drawn a thick, unbreakable line, and if you are with her, you will stay with her forever. If you haven't joined her, you will be safe for eternity, even though the end has not yet arrived. I see dark red paint poured onto the canvas, as if the artist were frustrated with the image he was creating. It symbolizes the blood of saints as they are killed and beheaded.

Hands stained with the blood of martyrs still cannot destroy all the faithful. Some are in hiding, waiting for the final trumpet. They are cold and hungry, yet they carry an unquenchable peace they would not trade for all the comforts of this temporary world. Love abounds among the faithful, and some have reported angels walking among them, protecting them as they sleep. Children disappear into the darkness, but they are not harmed. Angelic beings carry them to Heaven. Many miracles are reported. Food appears in cupboards that were empty moments before. Water is found in wells thought to be dry. Warm clothing and new shoes are left in bags at the door when no one is around. God is with them, and they know all is well, even as they suffer. They know they are loved, and soon the joy of the morning will come when the Lord breaks the eastern sky and takes them home.

08

The Path of Fear

Suddenly, as if guided by angels, I veer onto a different path, surrounded by an eerie silence that sends chills down my spine. There are no signs to guide me, yet something pushes me forward, something I cannot resist. Fear rises within me like crashing waves, but I cannot tell where it originates. Then, without warning, a sharp pain strikes my head. Its force is overwhelming. I can hardly think. I would normally lie down, press a cool cloth to my forehead, and wait for it to pass. But here, there is no relief.

I find myself standing at a train station.

I am waiting.

Panic starts to set in as I realize I don't have a ticket. I never saw a spot to buy one. Around me, others wait in line, each holding what I lack. The train's whistle pierces the air, loud and heavy. The sky darkens. My chest tightens.

What am I supposed to do?

How will I get on the train?

The train pulls in, and I stand there, empty-handed.

The wind howls, and the trees bend and sway. Something unseen pulls at my hair, and screeches fill the air. Rain pounds against me, pulling me toward a stream that suddenly swells into a raging river. Hands emerge from the darkness, grasping my hair and dragging me beneath the water. Voices surround me—mocking, accusing, saying I am being taken to hell because I refuse to be silent.

Fear consumes me.

I know I should speak. I know I should remember the words I have been given. But my mind is empty.

"Jesus!"

The cry escapes me.

And He is there.

He asks why I did not call sooner.

Shame washes over me. I hang my head and tell Him I'm ready to accept whatever comes, even if it means falling into the hands of the demons, because I have failed Him.

Then everything shifts.

The darkness fades.

I find myself on a different path, lined with roses that bloom as I gaze at them. My hand feels heavy. I open it to find a crumpled, wet ticket.

Purchased by Jesus.

He stands before me.

He reaches out His hand, and I take it. He lifts me up, and I hold on to Him. The fear begins to quiet, and the trembling eases. He tells me to rest.

I asked how long I had been lost.

"Two minutes," He says.

"Two minutes? It felt like an eternity."

Peace settles over me, deep and steady. I sit on a bench, trying to gather myself, aware that I am still on a journey.

"My child, some attacks from the enemy come with a warning, and some do not. This is a battle, and you can only prepare so much. After you've done all you can, stand in Me. Know that I am with you, whether you feel Me or not. You are saved by faith, not by what you feel or see. Through much tribulation, you enter the Kingdom of God. I seal you when you seek Me. I remember your heart when the attacks come. The enemy will try to make you believe I have forgotten you.

"No harm can come to one of My true children who is in My care, even during moments of weakness. When you fall, come back quickly. My Spirit will reveal what needs to be confessed. And if there is nothing, trust Me in the darkness. When you cannot see My hand, trust My heart, the One you have come to know.

"You will face many moments like this, where you do not know what to do. But I know your heart. You are in Me, and I am in you. There are temptations that come suddenly, because many fall quickly, and the enemy uses this. Turn away from them as soon as they rise. Do what you can to escape. And when you cannot, I will cover you."

This was not the first time Faustina had been attacked.

There were times when despair struck suddenly, pressing in right after she spoke words of faith. There were nights when she dreamed of abandonment, unanswered prayers, and being forgotten. Yet, just as quickly as those moments appeared, they disappeared. "O my Lord, stay ever near me as I travel on," she cried, rising again to follow where He would lead.

09

John and Daniel Meeting

"Daniel, did you see that? It was a train. A train. Incredible!"

"I have seen trains before, John."

"Where?"

"At a museum."

"When did you go to a museum?"

"You must have missed the new activity calendar that was posted. Trains were on the schedule. I plan to take a train trip soon. It looks like fun."

"Really? I love Jesus! He has made a way for all good things to continue. I want to go on a train trip too."

"Alright," Daniel said, smiling. "Now let's return to Sister Faustina and the fear she just faced."

"Yes," John said, his voice softening. "I felt for her. I remember what fear is like. Did I ever tell you about the time I was put into a pot of boiling oil, and yet I did not die?"

"Only a hundred times," Daniel replied with a friendly smile. "But I endured the lion's den, so we are even. Now, let us focus. She will be here soon. I sense she is about to lose more than she expects. She has already given much, yet the Lord will ask for more."

"I feel that as well," John said quietly. "Oh... there she is. Faustina, hello! You look lovely with that rose in your hair."

"Hello! I am so glad to see you and Daniel. A rose in my hair?"

I lift my hand and touch my hair. Soft petals brush against my fingers. I do not remember placing it there.

"That was quite an ordeal," John said gently. "Some enemy attacks come suddenly and overwhelm you. But when you give your life to Jesus daily, He covers you. The spirit world is real, yet God is greater than anything you will face. We are only passing through this world, and it ends well. I can promise you that."

"Faustina," Daniel said, stepping forward, "do not spend too much time fearing what may come. The Lord will carry you through. Do what you can today. Hear His voice. Obey Him. And trust Him with what lies ahead. There will be things you do not understand, and that is all right. What has He told you lately?"

"Well... the other day He told me He is going to reveal to me the plan of Satan, step by step. He said He would show me what happens behind the scenes, including what will cause people to believe in him and follow him. The mark of the beast is not just limits on buying and selling. It is because people will fall in love with the angel of darkness, who appears as an angel of light. They will prefer him. They will not care that he is Satan, because he will seem better than God, more worthy to follow. He will appear good, righteous, and loving. He will tell them they do not need anyone to pay for their sins, that they are already good as they are."

She paused, then continued more quietly.

"And then God asked me, 'What does it matter to you if I choose to have you alone with me to hear My voice? Do you not trust what I am doing with your life? I have called you. I am preparing you. I will speak to you. You must trust Me in this. I know you feel alone because of your family, but I have a deeper purpose for your life. I know every longing in your heart. Even the things you have never spoken. These things must wait. No one comes into your life by accident. No one leaves your life by accident. Come close to Me. Hear My voice. Grow strong.'"

John nodded slowly and added, "Yes. That is true. The challenge is holding onto what He has said when the trials come. The waiting can feel unbearable. It can seem as though evil goes unchecked, as though the children of God suffer without help. But that is not the truth. The Day of the Lord is coming. Every heart will be revealed. Right now, He is giving time. Time for people to turn back to Him. Do not mistake His patience for approval of sin. It is mercy. Deep mercy. Oh, that all would seek Him while He may still be found!"

10

Angel Wings

Sometimes, everything feels like too much to handle. I feel caught between this life and a deep yearning for what lies beyond, wishing I could escape the burden of pain and loneliness. It's hard to share what I carry. Few understand, and even fewer can offer lasting comfort. John and Daniel might understand, but they live in a different realm, and I am still here.

I am alone in the cave on this cold November day. Snow falls softly outside. I do not know where John and Daniel are.

Though I am still young, I feel the presence of age, as if time is moving toward me nonstop, like a noble horse that doesn't slow down for anyone. It comes for us all. The body gradually gives way to what it cannot resist.

We will all lose the world we know.

We have only known this life, one where we are loved and give love. And I wonder... where are they now? The ones I have known. The ones I have walked beside. Why does this loneliness press so deeply, especially when the world itself feels so cold?

Each day, our bodies move closer to decay. We try to hold it back but death remains ahead of us all. Many do not think about it when they are young. But I always have. Perhaps that is why I have always felt different.

I move closer to the fire, still burning in the fireplace, and a heaviness settles over me. Thoughts I usually push aside begin to rise. I know Thanksgiving is near.

And I am alone.

It becomes too much.

I let the weight of it take me, and sleep comes.

But it is not rest.

I wake in fear, yet I am not awake. I cannot move. I cannot rise. Voices surround me, familiar voices from the past, but I see no one.

I call out.

My mother. My children. My husband.

No answer.

The voices grow louder. Laughter follows, and suddenly I see a table, beautifully set, filled with Thanksgiving food. I can almost smell it—the warmth and comfort it brings.

I fall from the couch and crawl toward the kitchen. My small white cat follows beside me. The smell is still there, but when I reach the table, there is nothing.

No food.

No one.

Still, I hear them.

I call again, but no one answers.

Rain starts pounding on the glass doors, and a cold shiver runs through me. I glance toward the patio and see figures in white, but I can't tell who they are.

Then everything shifts.

I am seated at the table.

I am wearing a long white dress. My hair is thin, pale, and hanging around me. I wait for someone to notice me, for someone to pass the food, but no one sees me.

It is as though I am not there.

The people around me resemble me, but I don't know them. I reach out to touch the hand of a little girl who looks like me, but she doesn't respond. My spot at the table is there, then it's gone.

I am removed.

Again, everything shifts.

I am back on the couch.

My cat is licking my face. The heat hums softly as it turns on. My blanket lies on the floor. I pick it up and wrap it around myself.

I walk slowly into the kitchen.

I place a small cup of water into the microwave, adding a cinnamon tea bag. The quiet is heavy. There are no voices now. No scent of food.

I look at the calendar.

Thanksgiving.

I take the cup in my hands and walk to the patio doors.

And then I see them.

The figures in white.

They are leaving.

Large wings move gently behind them, touched by the falling rain.

I begin to cry.

"Lord... take me home. My heart cannot bear another day."

Were they here for me?

Will they return?

I do not know.

But I hope.

11

Mountain Path of Solitude to Meet the Lord

The intense feeling of isolation overwhelmed me, like the flight of a solitary eagle.

I stood at the entrance of the cave, not ready to begin the next path.

"Oh, Lord, have you forgotten me?"

"Faustina, look," He said.

I looked and saw the manger before me, with Mary, Joseph, and baby Jesus, angels above. Then Jesus appeared and said to me, "I have not forgotten you. This is where I remembered you." The sky above was filled with countless, radiant angels. I felt comforted, amazed at how quickly the Lord appeared and spoke the very truth I needed in that moment.

I wish I could say that I was then at peace with the loss of family and friends, that the cold of November no longer touched me. But the pain of solitude still lingered.

I've never experienced anything like this before. It feels as if I've lost everyone. George remains where he last spoke to me. I prayed to the Lord to keep him safe. I picture him turning into a pillar of salt, about to dissolve, but that can't be, because he didn't look back, nor was he fleeing a city of sin. I don't understand why he's frozen in this moment or why I feel the need for him to stay that way.

For a moment, I wondered whether to carry him up the mountain and sacrifice him on an altar. But that does not feel right. Why would I do such a thing? Is someone asking this of me, or are my emotions shifting and deceiving me?

So he remains there.

As I begin to climb the mountain ahead, I can only believe this is what I am meant to do. There is no other way. It feels like years since I last spoke with John and Daniel. They seem so distant now.

When I turn back, I see that the cave is closed. A thick door now blocks its entrance. Only moments ago, it held the Holy Family and a host of angels. Such is the spirit world.

I don't know if I'm climbing or descending this mountain. I have water but no food. My mind feels cluttered. I keep imagining donuts, popcorn, and bananas.

When I stopped at a pond and looked at my reflection, I was startled. Am I truly that old? It seems to have happened so quickly.

I brought my journal with me, knowing I would be alone. There has been time to write and to remember all the Lord has shown me and all the places He has led me. Still, I cannot help but think of George.

My food is to do the will of Him who sent me. I remember George sharing that scripture with me. When the Lord calls us away for His purposes, it is worth every hardship we endure. To deny the flesh and seek the higher things of God brings blessing, now and for eternity.

Pull me up this mountain, Lord. I am weak. Show me Your perspective.

For most of my life, I have poured myself out in search of love from a man. It is something I have never truly experienced. No man has ever fully understood me. What I desire is not only the love of a man but also the divine love of God. And yet, even knowing the love of the Lord, I still ache for a man's love.

It feels impossible, this longing. A quiet yearning that does not leave.

I understand my nature, yet I keep hoping and dreaming. I find myself praying that it will fade, that it will loosen its grip on me. Still, I remind myself that I don't need to dwell on it too much. My time here is limited.

I look forward to the day I will be transformed into His image. Perhaps it will happen on a mountaintop, alone with Him. The thought stirs something in me. There is no time to waste on earthly pursuits.

As an escape, I picture the joy of food. Cookies, donuts, pastries, bread. I've always done this, and my body has paid the price. The pleasure is fleeting. It fades quickly, replaced by craving, then heaviness, then a quiet darkness that settles in—something I carry and try to hide.

I will hike to the top of this mountain. I will find the cross of my Jesus. And there, I will die to myself.

I do not know His plans. I only want to be obedient, one day at a time, until He calls me home. The Lord showed me a tree. It was full of apples, but one sat at the very top. He told me that man will always reach for the highest apple. He will risk his life to have it. And when he finally does, he will see another tree and start again, striving for its top.

He will fight against others climbing beneath him. He will push them down to maintain his position. A man left to himself, without God, becomes a fool. His pursuits lead him to destruction, to a place where there are no more apples to reach.

12

The Path of the Faithless Church

As I climb toward the top of the mountain, the wide path I am on suddenly narrows. Is this the narrow path that all true believers are meant to walk? I can only assume it is, for are not all the paths that lead to hell wide and crowded?

A familiar scent of incense fills the air. It is pleasing, almost intoxicating, yet there is something beneath it—a faint trace of death. A wide variety of flora greet me—blue, white, crimson, and sunny yellow. Their petals sway gently, as if welcoming me. Nearby, I hear a bubbling brook and the laughter of children.

A strange peace settles over me, but it is guarded. As I said, this path seems right, yet something feels deeply wrong.

I meet many others along the way. Some do not want to be here, but they have no choice. Something is pushing them forward, fear or the threat of suffering if they turn away. I sense that many do not truly trust Jesus. They were persuaded to take this path because they feared losing their lives. And they valued their lives more than they loved the Lord.

With every step, horror waits for them.

And yet, the real terror isn't what the enemy might do to them now, but what abandoning the Lord will mean for their eternity. It has been so long since they called on His name. They have forgotten His love, His mercy, His promises. They have silenced His Spirit within them, having surrendered themselves to Satan. He intimidated them, and they obeyed. At first, it was fear. Then it became easier. When he said jump, they obeyed without question.

They loved this world and their families more than they loved the Lord. And now they are walking a path that leads to death.

This is a false path. It is narrow enough to deceive those who walk it. They think they are on the right path because it looks narrow, but what they don't see is that it only seems that way from their perspective. It is wide.

What a terrible place to be.

Fear takes hold of me, and I start to shake. Still, I put one foot forward, even though I don't know how I can keep moving. My legs feel like stone. This would be the moment for George to show up, but I am alone.

Jesus, please come to me. Help me.

"Keep walking, my child. I want you to understand the seduction that many will fall into, how they are drawn onto this path. It will be a terrible and horrifying journey for any soul who continues. Though their numbers may grow and, for a time, they may feel they are not alone, the outcome is the same. The blind lead the blind into eternal death.

"The appearance of pleasure will draw many, but in the end, it is suffering without end.

"Do not be afraid. I will help you. But I want you to come close enough to see, to understand how difficult it is, so that you may help them."

A bench appears before me, as if placed there for me alone, and I sit to rest.

Immediately, I see two lines forming ahead. One of the angels. The other demons.

The Lord's voice reminds me that the angels are under His command, and that I may ask Him to send them to help me.

The angels stand firm; their weapons raised toward the enemy. A heavy silence fills the air. No one moves.

Then the Lord reveals that I am a leader in this battle, here in the spirit realm.

I take up the sword of the Spirit. I aim, and I strike. I lift my bow, release my arrow, and the demons fall.

Then suddenly, a woman appears.

She is dressed in black. Her skirt flares out in an unnatural way. At first, it appears almost harmless, even inviting. But the mood quickly changes. What once seemed safe becomes overpowering.

People begin to understand what is happening. Panic rises. They try to escape, to find another way, but it is nearly impossible.

Her skirt spreads like a vast canopy. A force moves with it, like a powerful wind, pushing people beneath it. They feel they have no choice. They see no other way.

She offers them promises. Temporary riches. Fleeting pleasures.

But their surrender is not sudden. Their hearts had already been turning long before this moment.

And the darkness spreads.

The path ahead begins to fill with blackness as her influence grows.

"What am I to do, Lord? How can I help?"

"Pray when I show you those who are still calling out to Me. Not all is lost. I hear My sheep. I know them, and I will lead them to safety.

"Pray that they will find Me again. Pray for courage so they can break free from the enemy's grip. Intercede for them, that they may hear the truth and believe it.

"Many were called to be part of My bridal assembly, but they loved the world too much and became lost. This is the church that was unprepared for suffering. They looked upward, but only for rescue. They did not seek Me for strength or wisdom for what was coming.

"They did not search the Scriptures for themselves. They trusted leaders who themselves were led astray by false teaching. Now they are scattered, lost, and confused.

"They still call out to Me, but the words I spoke to warn them now feel distant, unfamiliar, even dark to them.

"They knew Me only as the God who answered prayers for comfort and escape. Now suffering has come, and they do not recognize Me in it. Still, I hear them.

"They believed a lie. They thought all would be well, that I would bless them here without trial. Now the trial is upon them, and they have no shepherd to guide them into truth. Their shepherd has fallen, or disappeared, or is lost himself.

"Many have lost faith in Me because of what they see in the world. They blame Me, forgetting the beginning and that I have already provided a way."

"Please, Jesus, I cannot bear this path. I hear screams ahead. Children who once laughed now cry out in terror. They are alone. They are broken. Their bodies are abused.

"What kind of path is this? What kind of darkness is this?"

"It comes from the pit of hell, my child. In their pride, men desire to become gods, but they cannot. And so they fall.

"But listen carefully, even though it grieves you. I came to seek and to save the lost. Even those who have given themselves over to darkness, even those who do not intend to turn to Me.

"I love every soul. But they must choose Me.

"Nothing good can come from a life lived apart from Me."

"Okay, my Jesus. I will listen for Your voice, and I will pray."

13

Word From Daniel

What a relief it was to find myself back in the cave with John and Daniel.

"Don't be afraid of what Jesus shows you, Faustina," Daniel began. "And don't fear the wait. Sometimes God's timing is a mystery, but His mercies are endless. Remember, He does not want anyone to perish, and His revelations are meant for our growth, even when we don't understand them right away.

"Some of His words stay hidden for a while, known only to Him. And you must also understand you don't have to share everything right away. Not everyone will grasp what you receive. Some will question it. Some might even mock it. But the One who gives the word will also bring it to those it's meant for.

"Stay close to Him. Listen closely. Follow what He asks. Prepare your heart to receive more. Let go of feeling the need to explain everything immediately. His plan is already unfolding as it should.

"He understands your struggles. He knows the emotions you carry, the loneliness you feel for your family. None of this is hidden from Him. And you are not alone in it. Others have walked this path before you.

"This does not disqualify you from His service. You will not reach a place on this Earth where you no longer feel pain. Some things must simply be carried.

"Let Him be your comfort.

"There is a deep joy still awaiting you, a joy found in hearing His voice, in turning away from the noise of the world and focusing solely on Him. You already know this joy. You have tasted it. But there is more.

"He has drawn you into His presence as one who is loved, called, and set apart. You have found favor in His kingdom. He trusts you with what He is asking of you.

"That does not mean you have not made mistakes. You have. But He knows that. And He has not turned away from you."

"Thank you, Daniel," I said. "I received what you have said. I needed to hear it."

As I sat with his words, I was given another vision.

I saw a great darkness and a great light covering the Earth.

Jesus spoke to me and said that the darkness is growing deeper, but the light is also shining brighter. Only those who are truly part of His church will stay in the light. Many believe they are in the light, yet they remain caught up in darkness. Soon, a choice will be presented to them, and it will be final.

"Many say they serve Me, but they serve themselves. They chase after prosperity, recognition, and influence. They want to be seen, known, and celebrated by others. They do not seek Me first; they seek their own interests.

"Yet they do this in such a subtle way that darkness appears as light.

"I am calling them. I am trying to reach them more deeply so they can hear My voice clearly. But many do not turn because what they have built holds them— their platforms, their income, their status. These things are valuable in the eyes of man, but not in Mine.

"Darkness continues to deepen because many who do not know Me have been given influence. There is still room for hearts to return to Me if those who truly belong to Me fully seek Me. But the time is short.

"Darkness is pulling away those who once knew Me, deceiving them with lies from the one who misleads. For those who know Me, the path of light will become clearer. But for those who don't, the darkness will grow thicker, making escape harder.

"Due to increasing disobedience and sin, many lose the opportunity to serve Me openly. Currently, the path to life can still be seen by those willing to look, but it is becoming harder to find each day.

"The path is found in Me alone.

"I am the door. That is why it is narrow. Only through Me can anyone enter life.

"My child, you have been set apart to speak truth about what is unfolding."

"I know you have not had a platform," He continued, "and that you are not widely known. But I can change that in a moment. I will bring you where you need to be.

"Do not concern yourself with how it will happen. That is Mine to do. Everything will come together as it should. The people you need will be there.

"Do not be afraid. A door will open, and it will be part of My plan."

14

The Neverending Search for Health

I found myself lying in a sickbed in a sterile hospital room in the 40s, unsure what illness had taken hold of me. There were no flowers in my room. No one cared to remember me. A heavy sense of impending doom pressed against my chest as I struggled to breathe. A blotchy red rash covered my body. I longed for a cool breath of fresh air, yet no one opened a window for me. I tried to reach for a glass of water on the stand next to my metal-rail bed, but I could not stretch that far. My throat ached with dryness, my mouth full of a thick, white coating.

Why am I alone?

Do I not have loved ones who care whether I live or die?

Surely, there must be someone, anyone, who will come and sit beside me as I prepare to leave this world. Someone from my church would be most welcome.

"Jesus... Jesus, help me."

In an instant, He was there.

"Am I dying, Lord?"

"No, but you feel as though you are, so you may understand the hearts of others in such moments."

"I hate this."

"I know. Ask Me to heal you."

"Please heal me, Lord... or take me home. I beg You."

Suddenly, I was standing before a mirror.

I looked at myself and saw a vibrant, healthy woman. My cheeks were flushed. I wore a favorite royal blue dress. My hair was brushed and soft, and for a moment, I felt whole again.

"Oh, Jesus, thank You."

"My child, this is only a brief reprieve. You will return to the sickbed. For you, the timing and duration will remain uncertain. Your good health will not last."

"Why, Lord?"

"So that you may understand what others endure, and so that your heart will long for eternity, where sickness no longer exists."

"Oh Lord, I will do anything to get well. I cannot bear to return to that bed. I will sell everything I own if I must. I will travel anywhere to find the best doctors. I will do whatever it takes to be healed. I must live. I must experience healing in this life."

"My child, this is where many lose their way. When the body becomes the focus, the soul is forgotten.

"I call each of My children home at their appointed time. I do not want your life to be consumed by trying to hold onto what is temporary. I want your heart focused on what is eternal.

"Yes, care for your body. Do what you can to remain well, so you may walk in what I have called you to do. But understand this. There is a limit to what I have asked of you in this body. I will give you the strength you need for the path I have set before you.

"I can heal, but when I choose not to, it's always for a reason.

"Some people give everything, even their souls, to achieve physical healing. Still, the body will fade. Every single body returns to dust.

"But what of the soul?

"So few consider it.

"They give everything to extend a moment of life, while the enemy blinds them to eternity. And in that blindness, the soul is neglected.

“Do you understand what I am saying?

“When healing is withheld, it can draw a person toward what is eternal. Otherwise, they might never seek it.”

“But Lord… it hurts so much to be sick. My body aches, and I feel so alone in that bed. Why does no one come? Where are my family and friends?”

“A servant is not greater than his master. I, too, was left alone when I died on the cross.

Can you trust Me with your life?”

“Yes.”

“I do not make mistakes.”

“Yes, Lord.”

“Then listen for My voice and seek Me first.

“Healing comes from Me. I have given wisdom to those who practice medicine, but I am still the source. Seek Me in what you consume, what you eat, and where you go for help.

“And when I ask you to be still, be still.

“Live for what is eternal, not only for what is passing.

“Ask for healing. Continue to ask until you know I have heard you. But remain open to My answer, whether it is yes, no, or not yet.

“There is always a purpose for those who belong to Me.

“At times, illness is tied to what has not been brought into the light, but not always. Often, I am working in ways you cannot yet see.

“Trust that I do all things well.”

“Oh my Jesus… I did not realize that even the pursuit of healing could lead me away from You.”

“It becomes the wrong path when a person prioritizes their will over everything else. When they walk without inviting Me into it.

"Too many live as though the body will last forever. They give their devotion to what is fading, instead of to the One who gave it life.

"Be mindful of the limits I have set for you. Seek Me in all things.

"Focus your heart on what is above, not on what is here.

"You have died, and your life is hidden in Me."

I dozed off with the soothing voice of Jesus in my dreams, only to be awakened suddenly by a shrill ring and a voice I had never heard before.

"Faustina, you have a visitor", a kind voice on the other end of the phone advised. "Should I send him in? His name is Saint George."

"George? Sure!" The surprise in my voice registered on the high end.

"Hello, Sister Faustina! Good news! I have been told that your testing was successful, and you will soon be released," George said with a smile as he pulled up a chair.

"Really? I thought I had to suffer more."

"Nope! You allowed the Lord to do what He needed to do, and He will not allow a child of His to suffer more than is necessary to complete what He was after in the breaking and making of the soul. You are good to go!"

"Oh wow! That is wonderful! Thank you."

"Not me, but Jesus. I am to give you a ride home. Are you hungry? Should we stop and get something to eat? I think a steak, veggies, and rice sounds good."

"Okay. Uh, when did you become Saint George?"

"I've always been Saint George. Oh, and here's a hanky that I have been touching. Keep it close if you feel ill again."

"Okay, Paul! I mean, Saint George, and please don't push my chair so fast!" she laughed, feeling more liberated than she had in a long time and deeply grateful to the Lord for her healing.

15

The Path of the Search for Love

Soon, I drifted into a deep sleep. I could not tell whether I was dreaming, seeing a vision, or if what unfolded before me was real.

The sound of music stirred me awake.

A new path lay before me. I found myself hoping, almost pleading within, that this would be the last for a while. I so needed a rest!

The dance floor shimmered under the lights, freshly waxed and gleaming. Streamers of blue, black, and white stretched across the ceiling, crossing above a wide canopy where white roses cascaded in soft, floating arrangements. Young adults gathered along the sides of the gymnasium, talking in small groups as they waited to dance. Some sipped pink punch, while others sat at tables draped in white linen, with bowls of pastel mints and mixed nuts neatly arranged before them.

The scene was beautiful.

And then I heard it.

One of my favorite songs.

A love song that had once made me cry as I imagined what it would feel like to be loved.

"You're every woman in the world to me. You're my fantasy... you're my reality..."

I froze.

It felt too real.

Why am I here? Why do I feel this way again?

I asked the Lord to help me understand everything He was showing me, to help me remain obedient, and to see clearly so I could write it all down and perhaps keep someone else from walking the wrong path.

And maybe, somehow, find my way out of this moment.

"Hello there."

The voice broke through my thoughts.

It was familiar.

It was George.

"What are you doing here? And what am I doing here?" I said quickly. "I do not exactly enjoy reliving these years."

George laughed softly. "This path will be interesting for you. Necessary, even. Many get stuck here. They refuse to move beyond it, clutching tightly to the fantasies of youth. It is a tempting place. You'll see that soon enough."

"But why are you here?"

"To help you find your way out," he said. "That is what a friend does. I will be the friend you always wanted, even if you did not have one then."

I couldn't help myself.

"Do you really think that highly of yourself?" I said, half-teasing, half-wounded. "Just because you were the one everyone wanted. You broke so many hearts back then. I liked you... more than I ever admitted. Did you ever feel the same? Mandy said you did, but you never asked me out. I never knew.

"I remember watching you at dances, always with someone else. Never me. It made me so angry... and so sad.

"Why didn't you notice me?

"I wore that blue chiffon dress with the small white flowers. I know I looked beautiful. My mother said I was glowing. I thought maybe... just maybe... you would see me beautiful too."

I paused, feeling the old ache rise once more.

"I am still angry, even now."

George shook his head with a slight smile. "You are already stepping into it," he said. "Apparently, I am *that* boy again. Come. Let's go.

Would you like to dance?"

"Huh? Oh... yes. Okay."

He took my hand and led me onto the dance floor.

My feet ached as they pressed against my white heels. Why had I chosen these shoes?

Another song began.

The words wrapped themselves around my heart, feeding the longing I had carried for so long. My dress moved around me like a dream.

This was it.

This feeling.

This was what I had always been waiting for.

George. My George.

Or at least, who I wanted him to be.

I wanted him to say it. To tell me he loved me, the way boys did in movies and songs. To prove it in quiet moments, on late-night drives, in secret places where love was whispered and sealed.

My friends smiled as we passed them. I had always had friends. I was friendly. Easy to talk to. Fun.

But it was never enough.

I wanted to be chosen.

I remembered my mother's face when she was in love—flushed and glowing. I wanted that too, even though I knew how often it appeared and disappeared, always tied to someone new.

Suddenly, everything shifted.

The path before me was no longer filled with light and music.

Dead roses lined both sides, red and pink, crushed as though something had trampled over them. And then I remembered.

That night.

The embarrassment came rushing back, heavy and suffocating.

After the dance, as couples began to leave, I stood alone, my white shawl clutched tightly in my hands.

"Ready?" George asked with a smile.

"Yes," I said, assuming he meant he would take me home.

We stepped outside into the fresh snow. We laughed, trying to catch snowflakes on our tongues like children.

He opened his 1970 Chevy truck door. As a gentleman, he helped me in because I was wearing a long dress and heels.

We drove through town, music playing softly, love songs filling the space between us. The streets were quiet, glowing under the dim lights. We drove up toward the water tower, then back down again, turning near the bars.

And then something inside me shifted.

"Do you love me, George?" I asked. "Like the man in the song loves the woman?"

He hesitated. "I have not really been listening to the words," he said lightly.

But I kept going.

"I would love to see you tonight..." I sang softly, tears slipping down my face. I wanted it so badly.

"Please, George... can you just say it? We could go somewhere quiet. I could show you how much I care for you."

"You are tormenting me," he said, almost amused. "But I think you will grow tired of this before I grow tired of being tested."

I didn't understand him.

Was he saying he was stronger than me? Untouchable?

"I am just a regular guy," he said. "But I know God will help me resist what is not right. I have other plans than just this night."

Still, I pushed.

"Just kiss me once," I said, forcing a small smile.

He looked at me strangely.

"Who are you?" he asked quietly.

Soon, we found ourselves behind the grain elevators, hidden from view. Other cars were already there. Laughter echoed. Voices called out.

"George? With her? Really?"

"How did you get him?" someone shouted. "Did you have to tackle him?"

I didn't answer.

I didn't care.

I was with him.

That was all that mattered.

We talked for a while about school, our teacher, and small things. Then I started to open up, talking about my childhood, my voice breaking and tears slipping out again.

He listened. He prayed for me. Then he held me.

And I didn't want to let go.

He tried to pull back, but I held on tighter, hoping he would understand what I was feeling, what I needed.

But he didn't.

Or maybe he did and chose not to respond.

What is wrong with him? Why can't he just pretend?

Finally, he said, "Let's take a walk."

We stepped out into the cold. The bars were closing. People stumbled toward their cars. And then, suddenly, I was alone.

The music lingered in my mind, but everything else faded.

Images flooded me.

Hands intertwined. Footsteps along a quiet beach. A beautiful woman, radiant and confident, loved completely by a man who saw her as everything.

She was everything I was not.

Her body, her beauty, her ease.

I pushed my short, tangled hair away from my face and walked on, unnoticed. My beautiful dress was mud-caked and torn.

Then the scene shifted again.

I stood on a desolate beach. The sky darkened. Rain began to fall, then grew into a violent storm. Thunder cracked. Lightning split the sky.

The rocks beneath me were slick, but I kept climbing, driven by something I could not explain.

Fear closed in around me. Seagulls screamed near my face. Distant whales cried out into the night. Shadows moved around me, whispering through the storm.

"Jesus, save me."

"Faustina, come toward my voice."

It was George.

The storm began to calm.

Soon, we were walking along the beach again, the sky softening, light breaking through the clouds.

I felt ashamed.

Ashamed of how I had acted, of what I had wanted.

I wanted to disappear.

George was gentle. He told me to let it go, but not to return to that place again.

"We are friends," he said. "That is all."

Then he looked at me.

"Have you really looked at yourself?" he asked. "And compared yourself to me? I am more attractive than you are. We would never be a good match. I could never love someone who looks like you."

His words struck me deeply.

Was he really that cruel?

He looked at me strangely and asked if I wanted to say something.

I wanted to ask him if he had ever loved me. If he ever could.

But I knew I wouldn't.

He took me home.

I fell onto my bed, overwhelmed with shame.

At school, everything returned to normal. Rumors came and went. Nothing lasted.

But the shame stayed.

I had buried it for years.

And now it was here again, alive inside me.

I wanted to run. To hide. To never be seen again.

"Jesus... please take me off this path. I cannot stay here."

"My child," He said, "now you see how I protected you.

"Many walk this path and do not return. What begins in a moment can become a chain that is difficult to break.

"Do not judge those who fall. You could have been among them.

"Instead of walking with Me, you might have been bound to the fleeting pleasures of the flesh. Come. Let Me heal you. I am the one who remains."

Overcome with everything I had seen, I pulled away from that younger version of myself, both in body and in heart.

I ran.

I searched for John and Daniel, passing George as I went. He looked at me, surprised. And as I ran, I saw another glimpse.

A future that might have been mine.

Worn out. Empty. Sitting in a bar, giving pieces of myself away to anyone who showed the slightest interest. My face heavy with makeup, my spirit drained.

I turned away from it.

And I began to realize something else.

George.......was not who I thought he was.

16

John to the Rescue

Sister Faustina hurried toward the Sirat Cave, tears streaming down her face and blurring her vision. Her sobs cut through the heavy silence as dark clouds swirled overhead, the air thick with the scent of rain. The atmosphere felt alive, almost fierce, as if the storm itself sensed the turmoil inside her.

The past clung to her like a shadow she couldn't escape. Memories surfaced unexpectedly of a frantic search for love, the same hunger she had seen in her Mama. A quiet dread took root deep inside her. She felt marked by it, as if something within her had already been stained. Nothing had happened physically, yet her thoughts and fantasies felt vivid enough to condemn her. In her mind, she had already fallen.

The words of Jesus echoed within her, steady and unrelenting. Yes, she had sinned. As all women have since we were born into sin. No one is perfect. And yet her heart still reached for perfection as though it were something she could grasp if she tried hard enough.

Her prayers had grown more frequent, more desperate. She kept asking the same question, repeatedly. Why does my flesh fight me like this? Why does it not grow quiet?

She did not want to become her mother.

She believed God had set her free, yet the battle in her mind would not loosen its grip. She could not speak of it. Not to anyone. They saw her as pure, disciplined, close to God. That image had become its own prison.

So she carried it alone.

Oh, what a miserable, unworthy wretch I am.

And this time, she would not go to George the way she once had. That part of her life would remain buried. It was too shameful to bring into the light again.

Still, beneath the weight of everything, a fragile hope stayed alive. Maybe John would understand. He spoke of love in a way that felt genuine. He walked closely with Jesus and believed deeply in His forgiveness—that even in darkness, love could still shine through.

She slowed as she reached the entrance of the cave, her breath catching as she realized she was not alone.

John sat with a scroll resting across his lap, reading aloud. Daniel listened intently, completely absorbed, as though each word carried something living within it.

"Now listen closely, Daniel. This part is especially good. And try not to pretend you're sick this time just to avoid hearing the rest of it after your last vision, the angel, and how you—"

"Just read, John."

"There are three lusts I wrote about in what you now call 1 John 2:15–17. Though I must say, I never numbered them that way. I do wonder whether Faustina has been organizing my scrolls." He smiled slightly to himself.

"Please, just read, John."

"Saint John to you," he replied lightly, the humor in his voice carrying something deeper—an understanding that all who belong to Christ are set apart.

Faustina stood still, hidden just beyond the entrance, her heart tightening.

"Three desires that stand against the love of God," John continued. "The lust of the flesh, the lust of the eyes, and the pride of life."

Her breath caught.

"These do not come from the Father, but from the world—and the world is passing away. The lust of the flesh is the craving for physical and sensual satisfaction outside of God's design. Lust is not love. It cannot be. It takes, while love gives."

Faustina felt the words land inside her.

"Even within marriage," John continued, "when the heart is not aligned with God, a person may act out of lust without realizing it. Sin clouds discernment and leads to more sin. Outside of marriage, it is clearly a sin. So how can it be called love? Anything that leads another into sin cannot be love."

"I know this, John, but..." Daniel began.

"I need to hear it," Faustina said suddenly, her voice breaking as she stepped into the cave.

Both men turned.

"Faustina," John said, warmth filling his face. "I had a feeling you would come today."

"How was your journey?" Daniel asked gently.

"Horrible... and wonderful," she said, her voice trembling. "There is so much to see. And I am not who you thought I was."

Daniel's expression softened.

"My child, we never thought you were perfect," Daniel said. "You are still in the flesh, as we once were. We understand. But tell me... has what you've seen begun to heal you?"

"Yes... and no," she whispered. "I need more. I remembered something. From when I was in high school. I gave in to lust, and I acted wrongly toward George."

"Yes," Daniel said quietly.

She looked at him, startled. "You knew?"

"The Lord revealed it to me. It is a heavy thing, carrying the weight of perfection. You were never meant to carry that alone. Confess your sins to one another, that you may be healed."

A flicker of relief passed through her.

"So... I don't need to say everything?"

"No," he said gently. "But have you spoken to Jesus about it?"

"Not fully... but I will."

"Then go to Him," John said softly. "He is full of compassion. Rich in mercy. He calls the weary to come. He forgives completely. He removes sin farther than east is from west... though I still wonder exactly how far that is. I tried calculating it once—"

"Not now, John," Daniel said, laughing quietly.

He turned back to Faustina. "Would you like to walk with us and pray?"

She shook her head quickly. "No... I want to stay here. I need the stillness."

Then she paused.

"What is that smell?" she asked, her voice softening. "It smells like... home."

Tears welled again, but this time they were different.

"Yes," John said with a smile. "We prepared some fish. Daniel baked bread. And we drew fresh water from the well."

Daniel stood. "Come, John. Let's give her space."

John nodded. "Perhaps we'll find some berries along the way. A cobbler might do us all some good."

17

Vision of Healing and Jesus

As soon as Faustina called on the name of Jesus, a weight settled over her, so heavy she had to sit down. It was not fear, but something deeper, something holy, pressing gently yet firmly upon her.

Before her, a soft green field unfolded, rich with life. A rosebush bloomed nearby, its petals full and untouched, as though they had never known decay. Then she heard His voice.

"Come up here so you can see better."

She obeyed.

As she moved forward, the scene shifted. Rows of hospital beds appeared, dozens of them, stretching before her. It was a place that didn't quite belong to heaven or to Earth, yet it had the feel of heaven. The air itself seemed alive with healing.

She saw herself, gently motioning people toward Jesus. One by one, they came. And suddenly, they were lying in the beds.

Jesus walked past them.

That was all.

As He passed each bed, healing flowed. The sickness vanished. The beds themselves disappeared.

Then the number grew. What had been many became hundreds. All deathly sick, resting in silence.

Again, He walked past them.

And again, they were made whole.

Joy rose within her. He had brought her home.

She lay down on one of the beds, waiting for Him.

"What are you doing here, my child?" His voice came, both gentle and knowing.

"Oh, my Lord... will You heal me too?" she whispered. "And... is it finally time for me to come home?"

Her voice trembled as the words began to pour out.

"My heart feels so sad. I am so alone. You see how I have been left behind. Family and friends... they have turned away from me. Some because I followed You. Others... they simply forgot me."

Her breath caught.

"During the holidays, I sit alone. No one calls me to their table. I would open mine to them, but they are nowhere to be found. It is as if I no longer exist to them."

Tears slipped down her face.

"Do they even care if I live or die?"

She looked at Him, searching.

"Isn't it time, my Jesus? Isn't it time for me to come home? It feels like it is."

Jesus sat beside her.

His hands came to her face, gentle but steady, lifting her gaze to meet His. His eyes did not waver.

"I know," He said softly. "I see every part of what you carry."

His voice held both compassion and authority, not one without the other.

"But it is not your time to leave the Earth and be with Me."

Something in her chest tightened.

"Your salvation is secure," He continued. "But there is still work for you to do."

He paused, letting the weight of His words settle.

"There are many who are hungry. Many who are thirsty. Some whose hearts have grown dark, hardened by deception. They need Me... and I will reach them through you."

The air around them seemed to deepen.

"Days are coming when darkness will spread across nations. A man will rise, carrying power that deceives many. He will lead them into a false unity, a religion that appears right but is not of Me."

Faustina listened, her heart both trembling and still.

"I want you to pray," He said. "Pray for those standing in the valley of decision. Many do not even realize they are there. They walk blindly, unaware of where their choices are leading them until it is too late."

His voice softened again.

"I know what you have lost. I know how it has shaped your heart. But none of it was wasted. Even your sorrow has been drawing you closer to Me."

Her breathing slowed.

"What you have lost is temporary. What I am giving you is eternal."

Then, gently, He added, "You are not as alone as you feel. There are those who stand with you, even now. But your isolation has made it difficult for you to see them."

She listened quietly.

"And you are already healed, my child.

"I want you to rise from this place and return. Go back to John and Daniel. There are still paths I must show you—paths that seem right, that feel right... but lead to destruction."

His tone sharpened, not harsh, but urgent.

"Many walk those paths together. To them, it feels like a celebration, like life. But it is a lie. And I want you to stand in the gap. Not by speaking to them... but by praying."

He held her gaze.

"I will show you the soil of their hearts. I will show you why what they believe has not taken root."

Then His voice softened once more.

"And know that when I call you home, I will be waiting for you at the end of a narrow garden path. And you will never feel alone again."

Something inside her broke... and healed at the same time.

"Go now, my child. John and Daniel are waiting."

As she walked, His voice remained with her, not around her, but within.

"Faustina, you do not need to strive to prove yourself. You do not need to speak of your gifts to be seen."

Each word settled deeply.

"In the spirit, you are already known. You have been given a place of honor, not by the world, but by Me.

"What matters is not what is built in the eyes of men. Not followers. No recognition. Not success."

His voice grew steady, grounding.

"I do not measure by those things. I measure what is built in eternity."

A peace began to form.

"I have called you by name. I am shaping you within My Kingdom. And your place there is secure."

She breathed in slowly.

"You do not need their validation when you already have Mine."

18

My Visit to Heaven

"I think you need to visit your eternal home, my child."

At those words, joy rose in me.

This time, the transition felt smooth. Before, it had been more difficult. I loved Heaven and wanted to be there, but part of me still felt attached to my life on Earth. That attachment had once held me back.

Not anymore.

I belong here.

Jesus said, "Let Me show you how paths appear from eternity. But first, let's take a walk."

Like a gracious host, He led me through Heaven. As we moved, He told its inhabitants that I was only visiting and that my time to remain there had not yet come.

Everything around me was filled with peace. Joy. Purity. There was no strain, no anxiety, no weight of Earthly worry. The atmosphere itself felt cleansing, complete, and whole. It was the place where I wanted to remain forever.

I noticed hospital beds there too, though they stood empty now, no longer needed. She knew they were there only to illustrate the power of Jesus.

"You will see many more hospital beds," Jesus said. "And many will be healed. Your part is only to lead them to Me, and I will do the healing."

His voice remained gentle, but it carried holy seriousness.

"When that begins to happen, refuse the praise of man. People will want to honor you, but with all your heart, remember that you are only a vessel. The healing is not in you. It is in Me, and I am in you. Hold tightly to this truth, for pride opens a door to destruction. Satan would gladly use it against you."

I listened carefully.

"Do only what I ask of you, and stay ready. As for where and when this will unfold on Earth, that is in My hands. You cannot force it or arrange it. I will bring it to pass in My own time."

Then His voice softened again.

"You are walking the path of truth and eternal life. It is also the path of joy, the path that leads into the beautiful garden of forever, My garden."

As I walked through the garden, one of the hardest things was resisting the desire to simply lie down and never leave.

There were flower beds everywhere, stunning in their beauty. They didn't look artificial or exaggerated, not like something from a fantasy. They resembled Earth flowers, yet they were different in a way I couldn't fully explain. They carried a sense of eternity. Everything there did.

And in each flower bed stood a small cross.

I asked Jesus why.

"When people behold this beauty," He said, "I want them to remember that I am the Rose of Sharon, the source of all beauty, and that they are here because of My sacrifice."

His words settled deeply into me.

"They are not here because of what they accomplished on Earth. Yes, there are rewards. Yes, there are places prepared. But no one enters Heaven because of their own merit. They enter because I have gone before them. I am the door."

He looked at me with great tenderness, yet with unmistakable authority.

"When they come to Heaven's gate, I must be first in their hearts. Not loved ones who have gone before them. Not friends. Not family. Me. I must be acknowledged first, because without Me they could not enter at all."

Then He continued.

"I want you to tell them this, My child. Many say they want Heaven because they want to see family and friends again, or even the companions they loved on Earth. And if those are not there, some scarcely want Heaven at all. This must change."

The sadness in His voice pierced me.

"Many believe they are going to Heaven, yet they will not enter, because they never sought My will. They never even asked what it was. They do not truly know Me. They know My name, but when trouble comes, they turn away."

His words were weighty, but not cruel. They were true.

"So tell them they must know Me. They must be willing to forsake everything for Me if asked. Family. Status. Position. Earthly power. Earthly titles. They must store up treasure in Heaven."

As I kept walking down the path, I felt increasingly at home. Every step brought a sense of peace and familiarity, as if something inside me had always known this place. Walking and talking with Jesus like this was more comforting than I can easily put into words. His presence was steady, like a light that never flickers.

Jesus had invited me into this garden before. Patiently. Gently. I had resisted then. But now I was here, and everything about it felt wondrous beyond language.

To seek Jesus on Earth is to awaken to the reality of Heaven. It opens the heart to glimpse what is ahead. Even if the vision is partial, even if it is dim, even one glimpse of Heaven's beauty is enough to stir a longing that never fully leaves.

But that longing calls for surrender. A person must lay down their own will and seek the will of the Father. Each soul must ask what that path means for their own life and answer while there is still time.

Tomorrow is not promised.

Then Jesus said, "Do not be afraid to receive what I show you as your own experience, My child. Do not fear that others will fail to understand. That does not matter. Seek only to please My heart. My presence will remain with you. Now go and speak with John and Daniel."

I went reluctantly.

I wanted to stay in Heaven.

But it was not yet time.

19

The Lonely Path of Being Unloved

I collapsed as soon as I stepped into the cave, tears streaming down my face as I sank onto the cold, hard stone floor. My head throbbed, and soon my mind drifted into something deeper, beyond the present.

John's voice echoed within me.

"If you don't weep in the cave, you will worship the crown."

Confusion cut through me.

"I understand the weeping... but what crown? I don't have a crown." A bitter laugh escaped me. "Who would even give me one? I was never meant for this world. My mother is gone... lost to me. No one has loved me since. I thought everyone could see that."

Then everything shifted.

Time slowed. My body grew older, heavier, slower. And yet what hurt most was not my body, but my heart.

I was old now.

My life was nearly behind me.

My children were gone.

They had cut me out of their lives completely, even after all I had done for them. They had told me I was loved. Told me I was a good mother. And yet... they left me.

Holidays passed in silence. No calls. No visits. No messages.

I could not understand it.

I had done everything I knew how to do. I cared for them. I taught them. I showed them how to live. I clothed them with my own hands. I held them when they were cold. I told them I loved them—repeatedly—every single day.

We walked together under the sun. We lay in the grass. We laughed. We shared meals. I thought we were happy.

I tried to prepare them for life without me. I gave them everything I had.

And still... they left.

They stopped calling. Stopped coming. Stopped wanting me.

Stopped loving me.

I kept searching my memory, trying to find where I had gone wrong. I cried through endless nights. I reached out to them, but they turned away.

And then... a message.

Cold. Final.

Leave us alone.

Stay out of our lives.

So I did.

And I was abandoned.

I woke up sobbing on the cave floor.

John was there, gently shaking me, helping me rise. He led me closer to the fire, placed something warm in my hands, and handed me tea. His presence steadied me, but the weight of what I had seen still lingered.

He asked me to tell him what I had experienced.

It felt so real that even speaking of it was difficult. But I told him everything.

When I finished, he sat quietly for a moment, then said,

"I can imagine that what you felt is a small reflection of what our Lord felt when Adam and Eve chose to turn away."

His voice was calm, but heavy with truth.

"He loved them perfectly. He gave them everything—freedom, provision, a perfect world. And still, they chose rebellion. They chose to leave."

I listened, my heart still aching.

"And even now," he continued, "their offspring remain on that same path. Many refuse to come home to the Father, even though He has prepared something far greater for them. But He will not force anyone. Love must be given freely."

His eyes met mine.

"Many will still choose separation from Him."

His words settled deeply.

"He has done everything necessary to bring them back, to offer them life... and yet they say no. He understands your pain, Faustina."

Tears filled my eyes again.

"Oh, John... I want to go home," I said quietly. "I want to be where I am loved. I don't belong here. Why must I stay? It hurts too much. It's too much."

My voice trembled.

"I have almost no one. George... he was my friend, but something feels wrong. I don't know who he really is anymore. I feel completely secluded."

John's expression softened.

"Soon, Faustina," he said gently. "The day of your homecoming is not yours to decide. It belongs to Him."

He paused, letting that truth settle.

"Most who truly encounter the Lord long to be with Him. Once you taste what awaits, this world no longer feels like home. But we are not the ones who choose when our time is finished."

His voice carried both comfort and firmness.

"You must trust Him. You must wait for Him to unfold what He has planned for you."

I lowered my gaze.

"Yes... It is difficult as he foretold," he continued. "But His way is still the best way."

He leaned forward slightly.

"Cry when you need to. Mourn what you have lost. You have lost much."

His words did not rush me.

"We all walk through this if we are truly following Him. Pride must fall away. Our attachment to this world must loosen so we can live for what is eternal."

The fire flickered beside us.

"This world is not our home. It is broken. It is passing. And if you find yourself loving it too deeply, it becomes harder to let go."

His voice softened again.

"It hurts to release the only world you've known... and the only love you've experienced. But there is a greater love unfolding."

I looked up slowly.

"And when it comes, it will fill every empty place. There will be no space left for the pain you carry now."

He held my gaze.

"Keep moving forward. And remember to look up. He is guiding you—just as much from above as He is within your heart."

20

The Sirat Path

After three days with John and Daniel, Faustina felt much better. Her brothers in the Lord had become a deep source of comfort and healing. She was grateful to share everything that weighed on her heart. George even stopped by one evening for dinner, and they talked as if nothing had changed. Still, Faustina felt uneasy about him, though she trusted the Lord to work things out.

Then, suddenly, she found herself in an old, familiar place, seated at a desk in a classroom. It was a beautiful setting, evoking fond memories of past times spent learning with the Lord. Daniel was teaching, with Jesus seated nearby.

"There's another path that mankind will take that I want to show you. The name of this path is Sirat. It means 'Straight Path,' but it is not. It is also called 'the bridge over hell,' yet it does not pass over hell; it leads into it. It is a terrible trap that many will fall into. Pray that they escape."

We heard a commotion from the adjoining room where the drafting tables were. Before our eyes, the number four drafting table was painted completely black, something I had never seen before. It was black, unlike anything I had ever known. It lay flat on the paper, yet felt multidimensional, as though one could step into it and travel to many places, hear many languages, and witness unspeakable events. I was in awe. I had never been in a classroom like this. It was an honor to be there.

Then suddenly, I found myself walking down a mysterious road. It was dark, and I could not see anything. I called out to Jesus, and He was there. I did not see Him, but I felt His hand. I sensed Him holding my arms, guiding me forward. I knew I had to walk this path alone.

Fear tightened around my heart, and a deep heaviness settled over me. How can I keep going?

I thought of celebrations with family and friends, and suddenly I was there in my vision, yet invisible. I was not invited to sit at the table or share a meal. I was hungry, but no one offered me food. I looked at the empty chairs and read the place cards on the plates, but not one bore my name.

"Oh, Jesus, is this my dark night of the soul? I cannot endure this. My heart feels every pain and loss I have ever known, magnified a thousandfold. The heartbreak of love denied and unreturned. The endless invitations to joyful gatherings where others rejoiced while I remained outside in the cold, gazing longingly at warm, flickering fires through frosted windows. The cruel words from family, each cutting deeper, how they called me ugly, how no one claimed me as their own, how they distanced themselves from me for following You. The betrayal of friends who cast me aside as if I carried a plague. I am utterly abandoned, Jesus."

I felt a wetness trickle downward and looked to see the blackness fading into a vivid crimson, the color of blood. The trickle grew into a vast, unstoppable river, expanding endlessly.

What could this mean?

I saw souls within the flow. Some reached the distant shores, climbing up despite the darkness that still clung to them. Others remained submerged, choosing to drown in the blood, refusing salvation.

Then I understood.

These were the ones being saved, carried by Jesus into safety, into eternal love and life.

"That blood is My blood, My child. Only through My shed blood can people escape hell's eternal darkness. Those who refuse to enter this river of My blood on Earth will not inherit eternal life. They will die and spend eternity in hell. But those who remain in My blood until their final breath will be with Me in heaven. Only through Me does one find eternal life. I am God, who came in the flesh, died on the cross, and rose again. The choice is this: to identify with Me and My shed blood, or to walk through temporary darkness that leads to eternal darkness. Choose My blood. Choose to identify with Me. Die with Me, and you will live with Me."

I was overwhelmed with tears as I felt the intensity of His love, real, deep, and undeniable, flowing from His heart.

Suddenly, I was transported to a magnificent scene in Heaven at the end of time. I was seated at a long, elegant table draped in a pure white cloth. The table was set with intricate plates, gleaming silverware, and golden goblets that gleamed in divine light. Each place setting bore a name, including mine.

Jesus moved quietly among the tables, His shoulders heavy with sorrow, tears streaming down His face. I saw the scars in His hands as He lifted them to His face.

My heart broke for Him.

Then He spoke, His voice heavy with grief, "They're not coming. Remove their table setting and chair."

The angels obeyed at once.

The empty places at Heaven's table were not given to others. They were erased, removed as if they had never existed. Jesus had waited. He had hoped. He had endured for as long as He could.

Now it was too late.

Everything around me dissolved, and I found myself sitting alone at the feast.

Then I saw those same individuals whose places had been removed in Heaven. They were now gathered at another table on Earth, celebrating Thanksgiving. Their table was full, laughter, food, joy, and fellowship surrounded them.

But there was no place for Jesus.

No space at their table. No room in their lives.

Only an unseen emptiness within them.

Oh, how my heart broke, knowing that His heart was breaking.

He made a way for all to live with Him in peace, joy, and eternal life, yet most will not come. Many will deny His name and forget the love He once showed them, as well as every blessing they received from His hand.

Those who reject Him will live forever with the weight of that choice.

I thought of a father or mother whose child refuses to come home, to love, turning away from the truth they once knew.

It stirred something painful in me. Even anger.

I wanted them to feel what He felt.

But then I understood.

By hardening their hearts against Him, they will suffer more deeply than I could ever wish.

And I grieved, for all the lost children.

Rebellion will end in hell, forever separated from the love they once knew and had taken for granted.

21

The Path of Ancient Wisdom

When I woke up and enjoyed my morning coffee with a splash of cream and a touch of sugar, the Lord revealed to me a vivid vision of five ancient men in Heaven, radiant with age, their long, flowing white hair and majestic beards shining. They sat in ornate chairs, each holding a book and carefully turning its pages. Jesus approached them and spoke with them, and they listened intently before returning their attention to the books before them.

The sight of these books stirred something uneasy in me, yet I could not understand their meaning.

Suddenly, a powerful wind swept through Heaven, and the men hurried, flipping through the pages as if searching for something just beyond their reach.

I felt the need for solitude, to reflect and to pray over what I had seen.

Quickly, I washed away the remnants of sleep, ran my fingers through my hair, and stepped outside, seeking the Lord's guidance and direction for what lay ahead.

To my surprise, I saw George standing there.

"Hello, George! What lovely roses. Who are they for?"

"You. From Jesus, with love, and from me too, my sister in the Lord."

"Thank you... both of you. And good morning. What a beautiful day this is. I had a strange dream and vision I would like to share with you, if you can help me understand it."

After I finished speaking, George paused for a moment, then said quietly, "I see the ancient men, and I think I understand what is happening. Look again... and listen carefully. Can you hear?"

"Yes... I can. The men are speaking with Jesus. He reminds them that those who are well do not need a physician, only the sick. 'I desire mercy, not sacrifice,' He says. He did not come to call the righteous, but sinners."

"Faustina, the wise ancient men are watching as you record your journey along these paths. Many who are heading toward hell are crying out for truth and longing for mercy. There is still time for the living to choose life in Jesus, but how can they choose if they do not know His mercy, the mercy that covers all sin?

"You speak of hell, and that is a vital truth... but now is the time for men to choose life.

"They need to see Jesus. They need to hear His voice through your words. They must know that they are loved, even in their sin, especially in their brokenness, their abuse, their hatred, and their pain.

"They serve Satan, and he is ruthless. You cannot treat them as he does—with hatred. You must be different. You must pray for them, even when their pain reaches you.

"They need to encounter Jesus through you... now more than ever.

"The purpose of His coming was to gather people to Himself and proclaim the good news that salvation is found in Him alone. Many paths lead to destruction, but anyone can turn and choose the path that leads to life.

"You need His mercy to remain on this path, and others need His mercy to begin theirs. So you must pray for them, not hate them.

"Pray for those who misuse you, lie about you, slander you, and do evil against you because you follow Jesus Christ, the Son of God. Some may still turn to Him.

"Bring them the roses, the red roses of love that symbolize His blood, shed for all mankind. He still weeps for the lost... can you not weep as well?

"Go to those on the wrong path and bring them the life you have found."

"Oh, George... I am afraid to go. They are so harsh and cruel, and I am small and weak. How can I love them? It feels like loving Satan himself."

"You are not alone. In Him, you find your strength.

"Love the unlovely with the love He gives you. It is not something you already possess; it is something you receive.

"He will guide you. He will show you His mercy.

"Some have seen His mercy and rejected it. Their hearts have grown hard, and their minds have turned away. Do not focus on them.

"Instead, look toward those who are waiting, those whose hearts are searching for Jesus, even if they do not yet realize it.

"Go to them. Bring Jesus to them.

"Many fear the final journey they must take. They are afraid they will not make it, for the path to Paradise is narrow and difficult.

"But remember this, even when the journey is hard, trusting in Jesus is the surest way. It is the only way.

"Some will stray and be lost, never knowing Him or trusting Him for salvation. But your role is not to save them, it is to share His love and His hope, and trust that He will do the rest."

I looked again, and I saw Jesus sitting with the five ancient men. Something unsettled me.

Was He aware of the hatred still hidden in my heart toward the very people He was calling me to love?

"Jesus," I cried, "what does this mean?"

"You have seen what I wanted you to understand. Remember, My burden is easy, and My yoke is light. I am not anxious, watching from heaven and hoping things will turn out well for you. I already know how your story ends.

"If you walk with Me and seek Me each day, all will be well.

"Stay close. Listen carefully. Remain in My presence until you understand your next step.

"Do not rush. Everything will unfold in the time I have given you on Earth.

"I see the end of your story, and I hold it in My hands as each page turns.

"Trust Me with what you cannot see. I see all.

"You will finish strong, in My name and for My glory.

"You are not alone. Look around you and see the helpers I have placed in your life."

"Lord... I only see George."

"Look again."

I looked again and remembered the friends who prayed for me when I was immature and lost in sin. At the time, I did not understand, but now I see more clearly that God sent them to help me hear, even when I could not.

"Thank You, Lord. I will wait in peace. I will seek You for my next step. Help me with my restlessness, my loneliness, and this feeling that I do not belong anywhere or with anyone.

"O my Lord, remember, I am but dust. It is only in You that I have breath. Remember me, Lord... and how weak I am."

"You are not forsaken. I remember you.

"And you must remember Me, what I have already shown you and told you.

Ask Me to help you remember."

"I will... and I do, even now, my Lord."

"Good. Come, sit with Me for a while."

I found myself on a quiet path, seated on a white bench beside Jesus. The fragrance of flowers lingered in the air, and birds danced in the trees, surrounding His presence.

Then George appeared, holding a rose.

"Let me guess... you've been giving roses away again."

"Yes."

"Can I have another one... a white one this time?"

"Of course."

"Thank you."

"Come and sit. Let's talk with Jesus for a while."

"I would love to... I was hoping you would ask."

"George! There's a worm in my flower!" I cried as it slithered out onto my hand.

"Oh, sorry about that! I got it!" He snapped his fingers, and the worm disappeared.

"Wow! Even the worms obey you!?"

"Of course!"

I relished sitting beside Jesus as we talked about life, eternity, and love. George was quiet, munching on a piece of dark bread he pulled from his pocket.

And then I fell asleep, resting against the strong shoulder of Jesus.

When I woke, they were gone.

But Jesus was still with me and always would remain so.

22

The Path of Temporary Knowledge

A library appeared before me, a lovely, ornate brick building with stunning white columns. Nearby, a garden held inviting benches, and a beautiful stream flowed gently through it. At first, I thought it was Heaven, but as I began to walk, I realized it was still on Earth.

I had always loved libraries, the smell of books, the quiet hum of coffee shops, and the endless discovery of new authors I adored. Yet this time, something felt different. I found myself above it all, perched in a corner on a small landing near the ceiling.

Odd.

I crouched low, trying to conceal myself. Why am I up here? I wondered. If I'm hiding, shouldn't I be under a desk or somewhere less exposed?

"Jesus, why am I up here?"

"So you will see."

"See what?"

"The passage of time. Look carefully as I speed things up."

Like a supernatural, out-of-control wildfire, calendar pages blurred past in a rush of months and years. The young became old in an instant. People, pets, and places shifted until they were no longer recognizable.

Children who once delighted in picture books now carried heavy volumes, their innocence slowly slipping beneath the weight of worldly knowledge. The harsh, discordant roar of early computers faded into memory as sleek, silent devices replaced them, whispering unseen influence into the air. Youthful librarians aged before my eyes, withering into frailty, then into nothing.

The grand remodeling of the library stripped it bare, leaving behind a lifeless expanse of dull whites and blacks, emptied of color and spirit. The vibrant garden was erased. The benches became stark concrete slabs, cold and unwelcoming.

Dogs that once wagged their tails on eager walks to the library now lie in silent graves. Their leashes and collars hang forgotten in homes that no longer hold life.

"When did it become illegal to have a dog?" the elderly would ask.

The children did not know. They had never known joy like that. They had only heard of it.

Inside the bookstore, beloved classics disappeared, replaced by new offerings that all looked the same, uniform, hollow, stripped of originality. It was an age where freedom of thought and expression had quietly died.

The people moved differently now. The patrons were subdued. The women were dressed in black from head to toe, while the men carried themselves with cold authority. At times, a woman's anguished cry would break the silence, only to be dragged away as if it were nothing. No one spoke. No one reacted. It was simply how life worked now.

The cozy coffee shops were gone. No flyers, no invitations, no sense of gathering. Everything was controlled. Predictable.

In the meeting rooms, approved lectures echoed with a single message: a unified vision of power and control, dressed up with promises of heaven for those who submitted.

Only the men smiled. The women were silenced, their emotions restrained, forbidden.

I watched in horror as everything unfolded before me.

"Why, Lord? Why are you showing me this?"

"This is what happens when man rules the world. It ends in darkness and the enslavement of both mind and body. Do not worry if your books are not well known today, for they will be tomorrow, when the world is made new and righteousness reigns. I told you before that no perverse or sinful works will survive the fire, when all worthless deeds are burned. But the books written for my glory, in purity and holiness, will remain. I know the heart of man. You can trust me when I say that what is written from a pure heart will endure. Take heart, my child. It will not be long now. Look again."

I looked again.

And I saw a new heaven and a new Earth.

Learning had returned, and it was filled with joy. People were safe. They were whole again. Love reigned among those who knew the Author of love. The air carried the fragrance of life, not death. Flowers bloomed where decay had once lingered. Harmony ruled.

Jesus Christ, the Son of God, had returned. And now, all things were being made new. The former things had passed away. Every pain was washed clean.

Then I found myself inside the new library.

I was seated at a small, charming desk, speaking with someone about one of my books. Thought and expression were no longer hidden or feared where Jesus Christ reigned. There was a freedom now deeper than before. A clarity of mind. A fullness of purpose.

Everything sin had stolen was restored a hundredfold through the new Adam in this new heaven and new Earth.

The god of this age had deceived many, convincing them that life with Jesus would be dull and that hell would somehow be more appealing.

"And if hell is not fun, then I won't go," they say, clinging to a false sense of control over their own destiny.

Such arrogance.

And yet, so far from the truth of what is to come.

All things will be made new, just as they were before sin entered humanity.

"O Lord, find us faithful as we wait for Your perfect plan to unfold."

23

Worship of Family Path

Firecrackers exploded all around me. It was some kind of celebration, bright, loud, and alive. The sweet scent of hot dogs and cotton candy filled the air, while the rich aroma of smoked meat drifted toward me, tugging at my senses.

Oh, I am so hungry. I need to find out what I am smelling.

It reminded me of hot summer days at the fair, where my mother baked and sold pies, always bringing home the blue ribbon for her rhubarb pie. I longed to taste it again, to go home, to sit with my family and enjoy those simple, happy days, running through the sprinkler, eating popsicles, reading books, and living without a care.

I had never stopped to think that it could all be taken away. That the feeling of being loved, of belonging, of having a family... could disappear so completely. I never imagined I would end up alone. No one around me. Not even George.

"Jesus, why must I be alone? What must I endure to be refined and used by you? I want a family, children, a husband, a home filled with life. I want to be happy, to gather, to belong. I cannot bear this! Isn't family what you are all about? You created us male and female and told us to go forth and multiply. I want that. More than anything, I want that. I want pets, children, and happy days filled with schoolbooks, sack lunches, birthdays, and graduations. Why am I alone in this world, where celebrations are so loud and colorful, yet I am on the outside, unseen, unknown?"

"My child, there is something I must show you, though it is heartbreaking. Many live only for the fleeting family on Earth, unaware of the eternal reality. They pursue the joy of togetherness, not realizing that everything here will pass away. All things age. All things decline. All things die. Loved ones fall ill, and often, in the end, only one remains—alone, tucked away, forgotten in a quiet room.

"It all ends, my dear one.

"They do not think about this as they build their lives. They hold tightly to temporary happiness as though it will last forever, but it is an illusion, one that fades. The time to multiply and enjoy Earthly life will come to an end. To worship your family is to worship the wind, something you cannot hold, something that will not remain.

"I am not telling you to abandon your family or stop loving them. No. Honor them. Care for them. But do so with eternity in view. For many, family becomes the center of everything, and they forget Me entirely.

"Only those who truly know me will receive eternal life. Many enjoy their families now, yet will not see them in eternity. Hell awaits those who do not know me, a place of despair beyond what the mind can bear.

"Do not worship what is temporary, even when it is a gift from Me. Be grateful for those I place in your life, but worship only Me, the Creator of all. You cannot carry your family into eternity with you. Each soul must come to Me personally.

"The empty, forsaken feeling you feel now is only a shadow of what Hell will be. There, no one comes to rescue. No one answers. No one hears. It is isolation without end.

"This will pass! The loneliness of Hell will not.

"Take a moment to feel this sense of abandonment. Allow it to serve as a lesson and open your heart to those who are lost. Remember, this feeling is temporary—you won't stay here forever."

Before I could respond, everything shifted.

I found myself in a wide, sunlit desert. A soft ocean breeze touched my face, bringing the aroma of crispy fried fish and sweet lemonade. It stirred something inside me—something warm and familiar.

I was seated comfortably in a lawn chair. A golden retriever lay peacefully nearby. Since I have always loved retrievers, I assumed it was mine, my companion.

George was there too... but something was wrong.

His face was sunburned. His hair was thin and wispy, as if it had gone through a thresher. A sword and shield lay at his feet. A few feet away was his helmet. He sat there barely moving. I let him be afraid to intrude.

But I wonder what happened? Dare I ask?

I turned my attention to another sudden activity; friends from Earth were here with me, enjoying the day. Their laughter blended as we talked about running back into the water to let the cool waves wash over us again.

The scene was beautiful. Peaceful. Full of joy.

"Thank you, my Lord. Guide me along these paths and strengthen me. Help me learn what I need to know and grant me the obedience to continue, even when it is difficult—when I feel forgotten and unloved.

"I know I am loved by you—eternally. And that is what I want to hold onto, always. But, Lord, I must ask, what happened to George?"

"He fights battles you know nothing about. Never assume he doesn't need your prayers. His friendship and concern for you run deep. Be a friend to him, even when you're focused on what you must endure. I have him in your life for a reason. One day, as My plan unfolds, you will understand how valuable he has been to you."

24

The Path of Worshiping the Body

I was on an operating table. Through the haze of anesthesia, I could hear voices saying I was being "fixed" once again.

I was old... but I desperately wanted to appear young. That's what the nurses kept saying. I overheard them discussing when they thought I wasn't listening, claiming I should give up, that I was too old, and nothing would change that, regardless of how much I changed my exterior.

These nurses, who had been so kind to me only an hour before, knew me by name and appeared to understand my situation and objectives.

Just a month earlier, I stood before a mirror in the hotel room in the city where I had the surgery, gazing in despair as the wrinkles reappeared. I knew the procedures weren't healthy in the long term... but still, this latest tightening didn't last.

And my neck...

I couldn't stop thinking about it.

To my horror, it had begun to look like a chicken neck.

I was confused. Disoriented.

How did I get so old so quickly? How did I even have this much money for so many surgeries? Who was going to take me home after this?

Was I married?

How old was I?

My heart let out a heavy sigh. It felt like I was fighting a battle that I already knew I couldn't win.

What if I died on this table?

Did I even know where I was going after death? I used to think I did... or at least I told myself I did.

What drove me to this? To become so consumed with my appearance that I would go this far.

Then it came back to me how I had always fixated on my body. On my weight. On whether I was fat or not. There was a number in my mind, and anything outside that number felt unacceptable.

But I hid it.

Inside, I felt empty.

Fragile.

Alone.

Jesus... get me through this alive. Heal me.

A mirror suddenly appeared before me.

And I froze.

Terror flooded through me as I stared at a face I didn't recognize.

Had I done this to myself? Had I changed so much that I had become a stranger?

There were other women in the room, admiring me, asking for my doctor's name.

But as I kept looking, I saw it happening.

Wrinkles began to form again. Slowly at first... then spreading rapidly across my skin. My body started to shrink. I felt smaller, weaker. My hair began to fall out—thin, brittle, almost gone.

Not my hair...

Suddenly, the room emptied.

I cried out, overwhelmed by a crushing sense of things happening so suddenly. I had to get out of here!

I grabbed my purse, pulling out my credit card, ready to give it to the receptionist for more surgeries, but there was no one there.

I sat down, confused, and searched through my phone, scrolling desperately through images of models. Perfect faces. Perfect bodies. Exactly what I wanted to become. Pulling out my little handheld mirror, I examined my face.

Just one more surgery...

That's all it would take.

Then everything would be right. My face. My body. My life.

Then I would finally be loved.

Maybe my husband will come back. Maybe he would see me again as beautiful and leave the woman he had chosen over me.

Where is the doctor?

Why am I alone?

Why is this place so cold?

What is happening to me?

"Jesus... please help me. Where are you?"

Then His face appeared beside mine in the mirror I held in my trembling hand.

I turned, and He embraced me.

And I broke.

"My dear one... eternal life is found in Me. I will give you a new body in the New Heaven and the New Earth. I restore what sin has taken. Until then, be renewed daily in the spirit of your mind. In Me, you will rise on wings like an eagle. The inward man is being renewed, even as the outward fades because of sin. Come... let Me heal you.

"You are not alone in this. There are many who will do anything to preserve this temporary body, resorting to drastic measures to hold on to youth and beauty. It is a costly trap. Even those who cannot afford it will find a way, chasing an image that will never satisfy.

"They have made their bodies their god.

"Driven by pride... by self-worship... by the need to be seen, admired, desired. They want to be the most beautiful in the room, and they will not rest until they are.

"For some, it is the only way they believe they can be loved. If they can just look perfect... then everything will fall into place.

"But it will not.

"Many harm their bodies in the process. Dangerous substances. Extreme control. Starvation. Obsession. All in the pursuit of love that cannot be found this way."

Then I saw her.

An obese woman is sitting in a pew during a church service.

She was beautiful... though she carried extra weight. And yet, there was something about her.

She was loved.

I could see it.

It was the love of God.

She knew she was loved by Him, and it radiated from her. It made her... lovely, desired in a way I had never understood.

I spoke with her. She was gentle. Warm. Full of something real.

And I realized something that shook me: if she had changed nothing about her body, she would still be loved. And even if she did change, that love would remain.

But I had lived believing the opposite.

To be loved, I had to be perfect in form.

And I wasn't.

So I believed I wasn't loved.

"My sweet Faustina... physical beauty will not open the gates of Heaven. That is not how I judge. I look at the soul. Do they know Me? Have they followed My will?

"Many will be shocked when they are turned away, believing that because I am love, I will accept everyone, even those who refuse to turn from sin. This is not the truth.

"I invite all... but not all will come.

"Time is closing. The door will not remain open forever.

"The enemy's goal is to consume mankind with the body, to fixate on what is temporary. Desires, passions, identity... all centered on something that will return to dust. Flesh and blood cannot inherit eternal life.

"The body cannot save you. It will fail every person who places their hope in it.

"All the care, the discipline, the effort, cannot stop what is coming.

"Even love between people, though beautiful and given by Me, cannot save the soul.

"Only I can.

"The soul is what lives on. And I will give you a new body... one that will never decay.

"Come to Me. Seek Me. And everything else will fall into its rightful place."

"Oh, thank you, Jesus... I love you so much. I want what you speak of. To feel loved because you loved me first."

25

The Path of Lust for Food and Alcohol

I found myself in a place I rarely visited, a bar that served alcohol, right next to a bakery.

I noticed the time. It was 2 p.m.

That felt... wrong.

I was hungry, so I reached into the bowl of peanuts on the counter.

The bartender looked at me. "Do you want the usual?"

The usual?

I tried to remember. Had I been here before? What did I usually order?

"Well... I don't know if I should."

"Come on, Becky. This is when your happy hour begins. How about a strawberry daiquiri with extra whipped cream?"

That sounded good. I guess my name is Becky?

So I nodded.

After that... everything blurred.

The next time I looked at the clock, it read 4:45.

My stomach ached with hunger.

Without thinking, I reached into the bag beneath my table and pulled out a sack of donuts. I glanced at the receipt. Two dozen.

Only five were left.

Did I eat all of these?

A wave of exhaustion hit me. I tried to stand, but the room tilted beneath me, and I dropped back into my seat.

"Cab's on the way, Becky!"

Oh… so I need a cab.

As I moved toward the door, I heard the bartender call out that he would see me tomorrow at the same time.

Tomorrow?

Am I doing this again?

"Jesus… where are you? Who am I? What am I doing here? Please help me!"

This path is dark and perilous, walked by many who exchange their spirit for temporary comfort. They seek false escape in alcohol, creating a cycle of drinking, disappointment, and despair. It's a carefully set trap designed to enslave.

"True freedom slips further away the deeper they go. What remains is bondage.

"And yet, for those brief moments of escape, a person will reach for anything just to feel alive.

"But alcohol weakens the body and suffocates the soul, leaving wounds untouched and emptiness behind. Without turning to Me, without confession and surrender, many will awaken too late, grieving what they refused to release."

As Jesus spoke, my attention drifted to the bakery next door.

I saw myself buying two more dozen donuts.

I knew what would happen next. I would eat them in the cab on the way home, chasing that moment of comfort. Then the sickness would come. I would end up in the bathroom… purging everything… before collapsing onto the cold tile floor.

Is this really my life now?

It terrified me.

I woke with rug burns on my face, bloodshot eyes, and a body that ached in every place.

And inside… I felt hollow.

Completely empty.

I checked the time.

Almost 2 p.m.

Time to go back.

To do it all again.

How does anyone escape this?

"Oh Lord… help me."

Then I was sitting in a folding chair, arranged in a circle with others in a church basement.

One by one, people spoke about their week.

Their struggles. Their failures. Their attempts to fight what kept pulling them back.

It felt like we were all learning how to be human again, like children trying to understand emotions we had buried for too long.

When it was my turn, I couldn't speak.

I just cried.

The room grew quiet around me.

And then… it was empty.

Only Jesus remained.

"My beloved Faustina… this is a path many fall into because it is painful to let go of the god of addiction and face what lies beneath it.

"Healing requires confronting wounds that have long been hidden. And that is not easy.

"Pain cuts deep. Loneliness lingers. Many walk this road without support from family or friends. Some have known rejection and carry horrible memories of what they endured. Others have grown up in broken places, carrying wounds they never chose, turning to substances just to survive the weight of it.

"I understand this fully.

"I know loneliness. I know injustice. I know what it is to be misunderstood and rejected.

"I have come to heal. To restore. To give life where there has only been survival.

"I can renew the mind. I can restore the soul.

"Come to Me.

"Do not hide your pain. Do not silence your emotions. Bring them to Me. Speak to Me amid it, and I will meet you there. I will begin to fill what feels empty.

"Those who do not know Me often do not know how to love others well. But I will lead you to those who do—those who will help carry you through healing.

"Look to Me.

"I am love.

"I call every soul to come. I make no mistakes in who I create. You are made in My image.

"Let Me be the Father you have longed for.

"Come. Let Me love you. Let Me heal you. Let Me make you whole."

I held onto every word He spoke.

But my mind still felt restless.

And the sense of falling with no one to catch me remained.

It lingered.

Oh, how I missed John and Daniel!

26

The Path of Children

I ran when I saw the path leading toward my friends—toward home. The Lord had answered my cries. Along the way, I met many new comrades who loved the Lord. They were also walking home, singing as they went. Many were weak and tired, yet their spirits were refreshed as they thought of where they were going. Jesus guided them over rough rocks and through dangers in the night. They loved the Lord and would not turn back now. Temptations of all kinds fell away from them as they died to self and began to live for Jesus. I was amazed to watch this happen. Tears disappeared, and strength returned to those who stayed close to Jesus. I wanted to join them and go along, but I looked to Jesus for His instructions.

"Not yet, My dear one. But soon. Go to John and Daniel. You are nearing home," Jesus gently whispered to me.

I hurried to find John and Daniel, but along the way, I came across some small children. They sat and played with a little white kitten, adorable as could be.

"Lord, what is this? What do You want me to understand?"

"These little ones are gifts from Me, the fruit of the womb. Many people refuse this gift, and even those who have children often treat them as possessions, as if they created them, when in fact their very lives come from Me, just as all life does. They live for their children, not to prepare them for Heaven, but because they feel they own them. These individuals did not seek Me or discover the purpose I had for them. There is always a higher calling in raising children, especially once they leave home a purpose that must be discerned. Yet many place their happiness and eternal joy in their offspring alone and forget Me."

I glanced toward the children playing with the kitten, but they were nowhere to be found. I picked up the cold, meowing little bundle of fur and asked where the children had gone.

The Lord grew silent. Somber.

"Those children were discarded before they were even born. What you saw was how it should have been, the blessing those little ones were meant to be to the world, but it was not to be. Men decided they were not human, so they were killed in the womb. Man playing God. Oh, how great will be the fires of Hell for those who kill the gifts I choose to give them! The torment will be worse for them than for the babies who endured horrible pain in the womb, their little bodies ripped apart piece by piece. I heard the cries. I still hear them. I create life. Before babies take their first breath on Earth, I have already planned for them. It is a gift from Me, children made in My image. Man wants to kill Me but cannot, so he seeks to kill those made in My image. I see the atrocities. I hear the slander all around. Anyone who murders one of these little ones will not be held guiltless. Mark My words! I know each child that was snuffed out by man's selfishness and lies, and unless they confess, they will pay with their souls for this sin for all eternity. The life that was not lived on Earth is now in Heaven. I will forgive all who come to Me and ask. But for the one who does not come to Me with a repentant, humble heart, it would have been better for them never to have been born. The babies who were rejected on Earth live on in My Eternal Kingdom, where there is no more crying or pain."

His heart was so heavy that I could only sit there and cry with Him, promising to do whatever I could to help save the rejected babies sent from God's heart to bless the heart of man.

27

The Path of Self-Righteousness

Many believe they are so wonderful and gifted that they do not need to come to the Lord, confess their sins, or accept His salvation. They think they should be allowed through the gates of Heaven based solely on their own merit. They have walked this path their entire lives, and now, at the end, they cannot understand why they cannot simply enter the path of life that leads to Heaven. The road of self-righteousness on Earth has come to an end, and they look left and right, seeing the gate to the garden of life. They approach confidently.

Jesus is there.

They meet Him with smiles and pride, saying, "Lord, do You not know who I am? I was very famous, very talented. Everyone knew my name. I starred in many movies. I was also quite wealthy. I gave generously to causes. Surely You know who I am, and I should be able to enter now."

Suddenly, the gate swings shut.

Then there is nothing.

They are forced to leave.

The path to Jesus is only through Him, not through pride of self. He is the only way. Still, those yet to come will not give up. Surely all roads lead to Heaven. That is what they have always believed, even discussed on their number-one-rated podcast, and their audience agreed with them.

But now they see that something has gone horribly wrong.

"Who is this Jesus they speak of? What a judgmental man He is to deny me entry! I hate him!"

Soon, they are joined by many others standing outside the gates of Heaven. They all traveled the same path. And now their life on Earth has ended, and eternity awaits them with nothing but their empty, prideful souls exposed for all to see.

I am not on this path, but I am near it and observe it as I quickly take notes. What a sad group they are. Yet they do not realize how lost they are, even now. Some are so bold as to shake the gates of Heaven, but to no avail. I see another entity approaching them. He is black and covered in red scabs. Strange. I realize that it is a demon, ready to take them to Hell. They can be heard mumbling, "My body, my choice!" as they are thrown into Hell. They got that right. They chose darkness. Then suddenly, all are gone, and I am left alone with Jesus as He appears again at the gates.

"Oh, my Faustina, it did not have to be this way. Men relished the gifts I gave them and devoured them. Pride overtook them because of their beauty, talent, wealth, fine homes, and possessions. In their success on Earth, they had no time to seek true success in Me. Now they have nothing. They built on a temporary foundation of sand, and it will not hold in the afterlife. They will hear no more applause. There will be no more movies to star in or music to sing. No one will worship them. No one will take their pictures or ask for their opinion. They will now suffer a great thirst that will never be satisfied and relentless hunger, with not even a crumb of food coming their way. They have sealed their fate. They believed that the eternity I placed in the heart of man meant they had control over where they would spend it.

"Lies. Pride. Lust. They consumed them all, and now it is too late. But it is not too late for those who turn and seek Me now. It is better to lose all fame on Earth to follow Me than to lose your soul in the pursuit of riches and the esteem of others. I have done everything necessary for them to live with Me forever, but they refused to come. They wanted to find their own god and worship the created instead of the Creator. A common mistake. It is better to endure lack on Earth, trusting Me for your daily bread, than to have so much that you forget you need Me."

Quickly, the path to life opens before me. Jesus smiles and signals for me to follow Him. I smell lovely incense rising in a beautiful cloud of white smoke, with candles on both sides of the path. He says, "I am taking you here so you will see."

A profound weakness floods over me in the presence of the Lord, and standing becomes a challenge. George suddenly appears beside me, his smile radiating warmth as he gently grasps my hand. An overwhelming sense of peace and joy envelops me, making me wish to linger in this moment forever. Yet, as I gaze into his eyes, I sense a depth of emotion I have never encountered before. What is it? Excitement, pleasure... and something else.

What could it mean?

Why am I seeing this on the path to eternity with Jesus? Such an odd sensation in this heavenly place. But he smiles at me once more, but for now, I will dismiss both what I think I might have seen.

28

The Path of Riches

One moment, I was walking toward a narrow opening in the woods, and the next, I found myself on a large boat floating on the vast ocean. The view was breathtaking, with a beautiful mountain range shimmering in the distance. It felt surreal to be on this majestic seafaring vessel. I sat on the deck in a comfortable cushioned lounge chair, with a glass resting on a small table beside me. It looked like juice, but when I tasted it, I realized it was a fruity alcoholic drink. It tasted good, even though I had not intended to drink.

I was not sure what time of day it was, but the crew rolled large carts filled with roast beef, turkey, strawberries, watermelon, and a variety of salads and desserts, all of which added to the wonder of the experience. Many people passed by and spoke with me, so I assumed I knew them from somewhere. There was a carefree air among the guests on this boat, and I soon found myself enjoying it.

This is living, I thought.

As I ate from the spread before me, the captain of the boat pulled up a chair and began to speak with me.

"Lovely day today," the gorgeous man next to me said, adjusting his perfect tie.

"Yes, indeed, it is." I pulled my swimsuit cover-up closer to my body as I noticed how little I was wearing beneath it. When did I start wearing bikinis? I had always been too modest for them, but here I was. And it was bright red, with see-through black lace.

"We could anchor about a mile off Ocean City and spend the afternoon strolling through the shops, perhaps dining at one of the local restaurants. I hear the selection is excellent."

"Uhhh... yes, that sounds nice." Why is he asking me?

"Good. I will tell the crew that you approve, and we will proceed."

"Can I ask why you need my approval?"

"Oh, don't be silly. We always get your approval for these tours, since you own the company that operates this vessel."

I was visibly shocked.

"Uh... alright then."

"Now don't play humble with me, Faustina."

And off he went.

I own the company.

Well... this is a surprise. I must say, I think I will enjoy this path very much. I must be rich. How nice.

A towel boy interrupted my thoughts, asking if I wanted a fresh towel and a drink.

I had not even finished the one I had, but I stammered, "Yes... a lemonade."

"A Long Island iced tea?"

"No, a regular lemonade. With lemons and sugar."

"So you are teetotaling today, then?"

"Apparently."

At this point, my head was spinning. What kind of path was this? Never mind. I loved it. I loved the ocean, the sun, the service... and oh, thank You, Lord!

I looked at the books on the table beside my drink. They were all modern romance novels, along with a book on horoscopes.

What in the world?

"Jesus, what is going on?"

Just then, I saw George. He was dressed in white swimming trunks, with three beautiful women clinging to him. All wore bikinis even more revealing than mine. I felt a small sense of relief about my own choice.

"George! Hello!"

"Hey there, Faustina. I guess the Lord wants me on this path with you."

"Yes, it appears that way. So, who are these lovely ladies?"

"I have no idea. They like me."

"And?"

"And what?"

"Do you like them?"

"Yes and no. They seem to want something from me. But look at that mountain range."

The women looked surprised when he turned his attention away from them. Not ones to give up easily, they began tracing his face with their fingers. One ran her hand through his hair, making a soft cooing sound. Their perfume was intoxicating in a get-me-out-of-here sort of way.

"George, are you being tempted?" I asked with a laugh, covering a cough at the scent that drifted toward me.

"Yes, I am. But I am no stranger to this kind of temptation. With the Lord's help, I will put an end to it. Excuse me."

He walked away, and the women followed. He soon returned wearing jean shorts and a T-shirt. The women were gone.

"So where did the lovely ladies disappear to?"

"I invited all three beauties to a Bible study. They agreed, though they seemed surprised when I brought my Bible and met them in the library."

"Oh, George... you have such a way with the ladies," I said with a laugh. "Now, could you help me? Sit down and help me understand what is going on."

"While I was at my Bible study, which was just Jesus and me, I read this verse: 'What does it profit a man to gain the whole world and lose his own soul?' So this must be the path of temporary riches and pleasure."

"Did you hear that I own the boat?"

"Yes... a new temptation, for sure. I know many spend their lives trying to become rich, only to spend the rest of their lives maintaining it. And you are doing the same thing, it appears."

Suddenly, the ship began to sink, and George and I were the only ones who seemed aware of it. Everyone else continued laughing and celebrating. A band began to play on deck, and more drinks were served. Guests were dressed in elegant evening clothes—long gowns, suits, and ties. The sunset was breathtaking.

The ship rocked from side to side as it slowly took on water, yet no one seemed to notice.

"What should we do, George?"

"Let's ask Jesus what He would have us do."

I heard, "Pray for those who are going down with the ship. Some once knew Me. Some believed they would always have time to confess and turn to Me before they died. Pray that their eyes are opened. Walk among them. When you look into their eyes, tell them that now is the time of salvation. Some will say, 'Yes, I am praying,' but others will ignore you and not even see you."

For hours, George and I walked along the deck, searching for anyone willing to pray, confess, and receive the Lord before it was too late. Most showed no interest. Strangely enough, I saw a large white figure walking with us. He was huge. "Do I have a guardian angel?"

We later found ourselves seated atop a high structure, looking out over the chaos below. The water continued to rise. Some people stood waist-deep; others, up to their necks; yet they remained unaware. Drinks still in hand. Laughter still in the air.

Those who knew the Lord lifted their hands in praise. Their bodies trembled from the cold, but their spirits rejoiced. They knew where they were going.

Then suddenly, the ship disappeared beneath the waves.

The ocean became still.

George and I stood on the shore. Gulls cried overhead as people walked along the beach, unaware of what had just happened. It seemed like an ordinary, peaceful day. George smiled at me, pointing out his new bright red swimming trunks.

I wanted to talk to him about all that had transpired, but he was off, running down the beach. My angel appeared beside me, and I felt a sense of calm yet confusion about George's sudden disappearance. I committed out loud to the world my calling to go "though, none may follow," once again to the Lord.

29

The Path of Hardships

I missed John and Daniel so much, and I was excited to be on my way back to the cave. It felt like forever since I had seen them. As I walked, I thought of a verse from Song of Solomon: "You are my private garden, my treasure, my bride, a secluded spring, a hidden fountain." Then I thought of Isaiah: "There He will teach us His paths, and we will walk in His ways."

But for some reason, another verse from Isaiah came to mind. I barely remembered reading it, so I checked my Bible to be sure I had it right. "You will blush because you worshiped in gardens dedicated to idols." Surely this was not meant for me. I felt relieved when I saw the cave's entrance just then.

After a warm welcome and sharing my adventures, we sat down with cups of hot tea, and I settled in to hear whatever the Lord wanted to speak through my friends.

"Dear Sister Faustina, it is very important that you are not afraid of what God wants to reveal to you. You do not know who will one day read your words, turn from the path they are on, and choose life. And please, do not be afraid of waiting. It does not mean you heard wrong, nor does it mean you have heard in vain. Often, He showed me things that would not happen in my lifetime, as you know."

John chuckled, thinking of another cave long ago, when the Book of Revelation was revealed to him. With a compelling look from Daniel, he quickly set aside his reminiscing and returned to his words of encouragement to Faustina.

"Some things take time. He is a merciful God who truly desires that no one should perish. He loves people. There is a place in Heaven for all those He calls. Do not think you have to understand everything He shows you. I did not understand everything, but He explained what I needed to know. You do not have to share all He reveals to you. The God who gives the word will also provide the wings for that word to fly. That is not your concern. Rest often and focus on hearing and obeying Him as you position yourself to receive more. There is always more."

"Yes, there is," Daniel said. "Faustina, He knows everything you are struggling with. He understands your emotions and relationship challenges, including the loneliness and rejection from your own family. He knows, and He cares. You are not the only one who has felt this way, and it does not disqualify you from His service. You will not reach a point where you never hurt or feel pain on this side of Heaven. Some things must be accepted. Go to Him, receive His comfort, and ask for His eternal perspective. There is more joy for you to discover simply in being in His presence and hearing His voice. Soon, you will long once again to shut out the world for a time and listen only to Him. I know you understand what it is like to find that joy in being with Him. You are greatly called, greatly ordained, and greatly positioned. You have found favor and honor in God's Kingdom. You are someone He can trust, someone He can call upon to do what He asks. That does not mean you have not made mistakes. I know you have. And He understands."

I was taking in everything they said when I suddenly found myself on a well-worn path. From the sweet fragrance, I knew a variety of flowers and plants must be growing along the path's edges. It was such a contrast to the darkness I had known, with its heaviness, loneliness, and endless toil.

Ahead of me, I saw the light of Heaven. It was clear that this was the way to life. I laughed, and eternal joy filled my soul.

"Oh my Jesus, my husband, let me always see this! I am small and unloved, a little bud trampled daily. And often I feel so lost when I try to understand where You are taking me and why."

Though the vision faded, the memory remained. The love of Jesus was always with me, before me, and within me. I can walk confidently, knowing that my eternal home is not far, even though the journey has been hard and dark, and much pain has affected me in body and soul. My trial on Earth has an end. Hurry it along, Lord!

I know not everyone chooses the narrow path because it is difficult. There is no applause, little recognition, much misunderstanding, and false accusations from those who should love me. Mankind takes his talents into his own hands and develops them as he wishes, without seeking the Creator who gave them. He takes the gift and runs, while the world applauds as if it came from him rather than from God. This time on Earth is a test. What will we do with what He has given us? Use it. Multiply it. But sometimes the greatest growth happens in lonely seclusion, when you are known only to God, not to others.

Many have pursued fame and fortune at any cost. They misuse their talents to seek personal gain, causing the gift God gave them to become tarnished, exhausted, and empty.

My thoughts grew heavy, and I lay down to rest. I found myself on a soft bed of roses when a dream came to me. I was outside the gates of Heaven. I fell to the ground, weak and overwhelmed at the thought of returning to Earth. Loneliness consumed me.

Jesus spoke to His angels, "Revive her. Carry her for a while. She is not done yet."

I looked up and saw Him. His face. His love. And His scars, especially His scars. They seemed larger, more defined. He paid the price once, and that was enough. I will live this life only once to show others what He has done and to urge them to hurry and decide before the door closes. Wedding garments must be worn to enter. Some plan to arrive in their own garments, carrying their accomplishments and honors from Earth.

I saw trailers loaded and ready, the wealthy believing they would impress God. Even now, they kept gathering possessions. Honors accumulated from their time on Earth. "My righteous causes should be enough to grant entrance, right? Right?"

They cried out into the vast silence as Hell opened to receive those who never took the time to know Him, the One who loved them, the One with the scars. They say they love, perhaps they do, but not the One who first loved them.

Jesus walked along two long lines of people praying. I recognized some of them. All but five had their eyes closed, as if in prayer. The five who kept their eyes open remained alert. When Jesus passed by, He told them to follow Him and said He would teach them how to pray. Those with their eyes closed prayed according to their own desires, what they wanted or imagined God wanted. Their prayers focused on themselves.

"The times have changed," Jesus said. "You must receive your direction from Me on what to pray."

I saw prayer warriors from five different countries—China, Norway, Germany, the United States, and a Middle Eastern country. I was among them. I followed quietly, because I did not fully understand what to do. I only knew to pray in the Spirit after asking God what He desired.

"Come," He said. We followed without speaking, trusting Him completely and ready to obey at any cost.

"Lord, show us what You want us to pray."

"Stay attentive to what is unfolding around you. Soon, people will say that Hell is not so terrible, that it does not matter where you go after death. You will hear stories of people claiming to return from Hell, saying Satan is kind and allows them to visit Earth. It will be made to seem insignificant. 'Live freely and learn as you go. Do not worry, you will have many chances to get it right,' they will say. I am placing the burden of intercession on you. The deception will grow. The church will be tempted to follow false paths that lead to destruction. Pray, My children. Pray that their eyes will be opened."

30

The Path of Imprisonment

As I waited for the next path the Lord would guide me on, I reflected on how hard it is to imagine all the good things to come. I felt stuck in the moment, thinking about how tough things were, how stark my life on Earth seemed, how empty everything felt, and how far I was from where I once thought I would be. But if someone's goal is to know Jesus and follow Him, maybe everything is unfolding as it should. It isn't an easy path, but aren't these tough roads what make us long for Jesus and eternity even more?

Suddenly, I found myself confined to a small, dark cell, with only narrow barred windows admitting faint light. Around me, I could hear the joyful cries of others being released, their freedom feeling so far away. I stood alone, unseen and forgotten, overwhelmed by grief for everything I had lost and everything I still longed for.

My thoughts turned to Pilgrim's Progress, remembering how it was written in confinement. On the desk before me lay a notebook, open beside a bottle of water. A small fridge held milk and orange juice, quiet reminders of a life that felt just out of reach.

"You are here, My child, because I need your full attention. There is so much more I want to reveal to you. I needed to create space in your mind and heart for where I am leading you and for the people who fill those empty places. This is not for anyone else to carry, but for you alone. The stage I have prepared for you is far greater than you realize. Wait. Write what I give you. I will oversee the release of these words at the right time. My words. My way. Rest."

I then saw myself standing in line among others. Jesus gently motioned for me to step out and follow Him, and I did. We began walking together. As I looked down the aisle, I saw George. We caught up to him and kept walking side by side. He smiled warmly when he saw me, and that small gesture stirred something hopeful in my heart, even as the memory of the cold cell still lingered.

Now I noticed the bed looked inviting. Soft, gentle cats gathered around, offering quiet comfort. They climbed onto the bed and fell asleep, waiting patiently for me to join them. Sunlight streamed softly through the windows. I felt grateful for these small mercies during my lonely journey.

I saw myself released from the cell, holding a book of poems I had written. Then, just as quickly as I was returned, receiving another book from the Lord. I saw my books lifted high, held above the rising waters. Then people began to see what God had given me.

Jesus spoke gently to me. "Trust Me during this time of separation from family and friends. When doors begin to close, do not panic. See it as being called away to receive from Me. Do not compare yourself to others, to other ministries, or to the opinions of those who have been used and prepared in different ways. Instead, look to Me alone for direction. There is so much I want to show you as the world changes and prophecy unfolds. You need to be set apart with Me. Do not see this as confinement, but as love."

If it were up to me, I would stay like an eagle in a chicken coop, pecking at the ground. But God has called me to soar, to leave what I know behind and rise higher, to places I would never reach on my own. The paths He leads me on don't always look the way I imagined. That's why He must prepare me. I thought it would come through open doors filled with light, but instead, He calls me into darkness because there are people searching for light, and I will show it to them. This takes time. This takes being alone with Him. Slowly, I am beginning to see what He wants me to see.

“Many will come to know Me because of your testimony. But where I am taking you carries weight, and you must hear My voice clearly and obey.”

I saw two people sitting on my bed, and the number two was written on the front of my notebook. The same number appeared again on the window. Then I saw the Lord breathe, and suddenly I was standing on the Earth, reading from the pages of my book. The pages lifted and moved with His breath, traveling to different places. I would read, and then I would find myself somewhere else, as the words went wherever God sent them.

Jesus showed me that He can raise a man from the dust to fulfill His purposes. I am to wait. The time appointed for what God has ordained will come, and nothing I do will undo it as long as I continue seeking Him. I will be strengthened. I will be healed. There will come a time when I will no longer depend on others to take me where He is leading me. The right people will be there when needed.

God showed me that things are changing. It is not His plan to keep me hidden forever. But for now, He is calling me to Himself. I will feel confined by His love, but it is in that place that I will hear His voice clearly, seek His face, and intercede. I will not always remain unknown. It is not over for me. God will provide for my needs. He has given me words and stories to share with His people. It is not yet time for me to go home to Heaven. There is still work to be done.

He will enable me to fulfill the calling He has placed on my life. He knows what I need. He understands who I am and how easily I can lose my way. When success comes, He will lead me back to Him for every next step. This is not punishment. It is protection. Not one of the purposes He has for me will be forgotten. The times I feel held in this place will become the very words I share with others one day.

The door is not locked. I have a choice: to remain still in His presence or to rise and move. But even when I move, I can remain with Him.

31

The Death Path of the Antichrist Spirit

Two rows appear before me, one of demons rendered powerless in Jesus' name, and another of obedient, radiant angels. I understand that I cannot command angels, yet I wonder what this means. God reveals that demons are attempting to corrupt even those who appear to serve Him, disguising themselves as angels and concealing their true nature behind a flutter of wings. Many are led to believe they are safe, that God is with them.

These are demons posing as pure, innocent angels, deceptively aligned with God. Many high-profile leaders are deceived, elevating themselves and demanding God's intervention without truly seeking His will.

Amid this, I see a golden figure resembling Jesus, yet it is the Antichrist in disguise. Beneath its shining surface, darkness grows, upheld by demonic forces. Rays of gold shine from it, but as it is manipulated, it turns black, blinding the masses.

Unknowingly, people worship this false image, bowing down and hiding themselves. Those who refuse to worship the Antichrist will face violence. The danger is hidden because he appears harmless and safe. But those who truly seek the Lord will be given eyes to see beyond the disguise.

Black venom pours from the Antichrist's mouth and spreads across the land. The stage is being set for him to rule.

As I watch this unfold, I hear the Lord's voice calling me higher, to see from Heaven's perspective. He tells me that from there, I will see the path more clearly. I feel confused about John and Daniel, because I know they are on Earth with me, yet they are also in eternity. I know I am still on Earth, only being allowed to see beyond it.

"What do You want to show me, Father?"

"I want to show you how easily people are drawn onto the wide path that leads to destruction. Satan tempts those whose minds are idle and whose lives lack purpose. Man carries eternity within him yet lives as though both body and soul will remain forever. That is the danger. Many do not believe the flesh will pass away, and that only the soul will stand before Me.

'The road of self-worship is wide and appealing. At first, it feels pleasant because it offers endless satisfaction. Do what feels good. Follow your desires. It is your life. Live it as you choose. No one can stop you. You decide what is right for you. You can do what you want with your body.

"But suddenly, on this road of self-fulfillment, your soul is required of you. Because of the pursuit of pleasure, you place yourself in danger. You expose yourself to things that lead to destruction, and in a moment, your soul stands before Me, uncovered.

"The path to self-glorification often begins subtly, hidden beneath the appearance of freedom and pride. As possessions increase, as wealth grows, as power is gained, and as others' approval rises, it becomes easier to believe that this life is all there is.

"As temporary success increases, pride takes hold. I did this. I earned this. I am in control. And now I will enjoy what I have built.

"But the road to self-fulfillment always ends in death. Many arrive at the end in deep sorrow, because it is too late to seek the higher purpose, to know Me, the One who created them."

I see this all around me, this spirit spreading. I feel convicted, not because I have possessions or wealth, but because I, too, have lived for myself, focused only on the present, without thought for eternity.

The path the Lord has placed me on is difficult and lonely, yes, but I now see how much of my life has been centered on myself. It is hard to surrender when everything must be about Jesus.

"O Lord, I am sorry!"

"My Faustina, the time of evil on Earth will be brief. Compared to eternity, it is only a moment. Tell them this, Faustina. Many are discouraged, just as you are. They are tired. I see how you have labored, how much you have written, and all that you have seen. I see your desire to share it.

"It is all in My timing. The words I have given you will reach those who need them at the appointed time. Not everyone is ready, but those who will find what I have given you.

"Do not rely on human messengers. They are often driven by temporary success and popularity. The words I give are eternal. They will remain. This is My work. You are My servant.

"All have had to wait for what I have spoken to come to pass. You are no different. Wait patiently, and you will be rewarded when My sons and daughters are revealed."

32

The Cares of Life Road

The next day, to my surprise, I woke peacefully in my bed at home. After a quick breakfast, during which I saw no one, I set out again. I felt restless. I did not want to leave, but I also did not want to stay. The journey was wearing me down. There were still things waiting for me at home, like feeding my four cats. They seemed fine, though just as round as ever.

Ah, perfect, I thought, as I saw a sign that read, "The Cares of Life Road." So many things to think about on this road. Important things. Necessary things. You are just trying to take care of yourself, right? Trying to survive. Trying to help others along the way.

Everything that needed to be done for our day-to-day lives was handled and consumed, leaving hardly a moment to think about the future. But even thinking about the future becomes its own burden, because how does one prepare for something that may never come? Yet, like the path of self, the Cares of Life Road can lead to destruction. It appears to be righteous, concerned for the needy, fundraising for temporary needs, and promoting worthy causes. But an excessive focus on the temporary becomes dangerous.

Satan whispers into the minds of those consumed by the present, telling them that this is all there is. They must act now. That everything depends on what they do today. Not that these things are wrong in themselves, but they become harmful when they become everything. They become empty when the Lord is no longer the reason behind them.

They become like seeds scattered on the surface, never planted, never rooted, carried away by the wind before they can grow.

This mindset shows itself in excessive concern for family, as though life on Earth will last forever. Constant planning. Constant worry over physical well-being, while spiritual health is neglected. Yes, caring for your family is important. But when your focus remains only on this life, it leads to spiritual death.

I suddenly found myself hidden in someone's kitchen. No one could see me, but I saw and heard everything. A couple sat at the table early in the morning, drinking coffee and eating blueberry scones. My mouth watered at the sight of them.

"Can we get Spencer out of school early in December so we can board a plane to Greece for Christmas?" asked a well-dressed man in his late thirties.

"I will ask today," replied an equally polished woman, her honey-blonde hair pulled into a neat bun.

"And will your parents be available to watch the house and feed our pets?"

"I'm sure they will be. Daddy should have recovered from his surgery by then."

"Oh, right. I forgot about that."

"Are you working on that project with Andrew today?"

"The Miller Mansion Project? Yes."

"Andrew will think you look especially beautiful today."

"Stop it. We are just friends."

"He doesn't look at you like you are just friends. At the Christmas party last year, he was watching you closely."

"So? He does that with many women. I must go." She glanced at the clock. "Goodbye. Love you."

Della gave Mitch a quick kiss, grabbed her keys, and left.

"Lord," I asked, "what do You want me to see here?"

"Keep watching."

Mitch grabbed his keys and headed to the garage, climbing into his custom light-blue Jaguar. His reward for years of work and success as a broker. He knew his marriage had suffered from long hours and constant travel, but he believed it was necessary. Della and the children benefited from his success.

As he backed out, he glanced at his perfectly kept lawn, with a golf course just a mile away. He called his assistant to say he would be a little late but would make his ten o'clock meeting.

He slowed down, keeping his distance from Della. He wanted to know why she seemed different and following her seemed the best way to find out.

When she arrived at her design studio, everything became clear. The new hire, with his sculpted looks and confident demeanor, was already there. He met her just out of sight by the large tree and kissed her. Then they got into his car and drove off.

Mitch followed them to a nearby hotel. Ninety minutes later, everything erupted. A confrontation. A punch. Police.

Della shouted at him, saying he had humiliated her. She wanted a divorce.

"I beat you to it. The papers will be ready this afternoon."

The months that followed were filled with lawyers, sales, new living arrangements, arguments, and endless tears. When the divorce was final, Mitch swore he would never love again and turned to drinking. Della moved in with her new partner and refused to commit again. The children moved between homes, often sent away to schools, camps, or relatives. The burdens of life had quietly destroyed them. God had never been part of it. Everything had been driven by survival, with each person looking only after themselves.

I then found myself standing in a cemetery during a burial. I heard whispers about what a good man he had been, and how tragic it was. A woman stood at a distance, dressed in black, her face hidden behind dark glasses. Two young adults stood by the grave, weeping.

"Who died, Jesus?"

"Mitch. He was overwhelmed by life's burdens, trying to repair his broken soul in his own way. His efforts were in vain. He never came to Me on Earth, and now he will meet Me only once more, in eternity, and face judgment for rejecting Me. He had a choice, but he chose wrongly.

"All who are born will face this same decision. It cannot be postponed, because tomorrow is not promised. The cares of life will always be there, but the door to salvation will not remain open forever. The opportunity will pass. Today is the day of salvation, yet many will perish because they ignore it."

I understood what the Lord was showing me. I had often thought about how short life is, how suddenly it can end. Everyone has a story, from beginning to end. Some are given time to choose. Others are not. Some carry sorrow daily. Others live with ease, never questioning what lies ahead.

But God is just. He will judge rightly. Those who call on Him will be with Him forever, where sorrow and pain are no more, and where they will never again question whether they are loved.

33
The Path to Hell

"The Cares of Life Road" was both fascinating and tragic to witness. I explained everything to John and Daniel. They understood what I was going through and explained how the Word of God fits into every historical period. As we talked, I mentioned that my journey was speeding up, with rapid transitions.

John shared this wisdom: "It symbolizes the urgency of the present. Even if the Lord tarries, many will take their last breath. Multitudes are on the Path to Hell for the way is wide."

"Yes, and speaking of that, I hear the Lord calling me. Pray for me. I feel apprehensive."

Thunder booms in the distance as the sky darkens, and daylight rapidly fades, replaced by the scent of approaching rain. Usually, I find the smell of rain refreshing, but today it feels different. The spiritual light has long since dimmed, yet few seem to notice the loss. Suddenly, a chilly wind erupts, howling fiercely and hurling dead branches into the air, while icy fingers seem to scrape at the window of my soul. In that moment, I fall as the Lord's presence overwhelms me.

I lie still for what feels like hours, too afraid to get up, yet Jesus is calling me. An angel is ready to help. I can barely stand, but I must obey. I need to see what the Lord wants to reveal. What I witness shocks me. Many happily walk this path without fear of what's ahead because they do not believe in a place called Hell. They think that even if such a place existed, the God of Love described by Christians would neither send nor keep anyone there. They mistakenly believe that Jesus's coming means there is no eternal punishment for anyone, forgetting that one must believe and be born again to receive eternal life. If they care at all, they will know and heed His words that it would be better to enter life maimed or crippled or with one eye than to have your whole body thrown into an everlasting fire where your worm does not die. They wrongly believe that Hell is merely a metaphor, but that is not what Jesus said.

"Don't all roads eventually lead to the same destination? Eternal happiness, a place of free will, where whatever you desire is fulfilled, and whoever you want is there with you. A place where every dream comes true, and you are reunited with all those who have gone before. Popular and wealthy celebrities claim this is so," they reassure themselves.

"Why, Lord? Why don't they believe?"

"The great deceiver, Satan, the Prince of the Power of the Air, has deceived them. He has lied, telling them they have time and that eternity is nothing to worry about. The growing darkness of Earth is not enough to make them feel a sense of urgency. They think that since life continues as it always has, there's no reason for anything to change—believing they will have control over their destiny in the hereafter just as they do on Earth.

"Men think they are finding their way okay with their own small light, not realizing that their lives can end suddenly, leaving them with no control over their actions or destination. They will face eternity without any cover for their sins. I cannot tolerate sin when I paid the price for everyone to be free from it, but not everyone accepts this gift.

"And you, Faustina, will shine for Me in the darkness, but not yet. It is not dark enough. No one would bother to heed your warnings. If I opened a great, effective door now, no one would notice because they are still walking in their own light. They are not afraid of Hell because their pride convinces them it is not real. Some even mock Me, saying Hell will be fun, and ask to visit. They speak arrogantly because the light of this world still shines brightly, and they believe it always will. But it will not, for I am the light, and suddenly, everything will go dark. They are serving the God of this world, Satan. He lies to them all day and night, but they sense no danger because their hearts have become cold and hardened. They have ignored My quiet, gentle whisper. There is no fear of Me in their hearts. They do not fear death either, because Satan lies and tells them not to worry about it, to avoid negativity, live for today, enjoy yourself, you only go around once, so keep going and having fun. They seek to pleasure themselves and do not worry about eternity."

"Prepare me for what you want me to see next, my Lord," my voice trembling with anxiety. I cannot evade what Jesus is trying to reveal to me or where He plans to lead, so I surrender and wait for His guidance.

I sit beside a massive black rock at the entrance of a wide path and close my eyes. Suddenly, I am engulfed by darkness. A wave of faintness floods over me, and I struggle to breathe as the darkness surrounds me—

darker than any place I have ever known—darker than a deserted country road under a pitch-black sky, with not a single light from a distant farmhouse. Darkness more profound than the deepest pit one could fall into, or a cave with no torch to light the way. Darkness that far exceeds physical blindness. I find myself in a despairing abyss, more suffocating than the most bottomless pit and more terrifying than the cruelest torture conceived by evil. It is a place where screams echo endlessly into the void, unheard, and pain never ends. A place haunted by the horrors of the past, for all light, joy, and goodness have disappeared—they originate in Jesus and are accessible only to those who know and love Him. People have little understanding of how truly terrible it is. Nothing on Earth can prepare you for Hell. Nothing compares, and nothing ever will.

I am overwhelmed with visions of children, now grown, who have rebelled against the God of their youth, now controlled by a complete lack of empathy, total indifference to the cry of those who gave them life. Children are walking mindlessly into the very gates of Hell. There are cheers of encouragement all around them to rebel, live your own life, your parents do not understand you, cut them off, they are abusive. Though abuse does happen, this group of parents are not abusers.

What a terrible time this is! I feel the pain of the parents who faithfully pray and would welcome the prodigal home, if only they'd turn around.

"Uplift the parents, Lord. Tell them not to give up praying, and may it not be too late!"

34

The Path of Trusting the Government

I wander through the night, hoping I am on the right path back to the cave, to John and Daniel. I weep as I walk. Jesus speaks to me from the shadows, His voice carrying healing light into my soul.

"I'm preparing you for promotion in the spiritual realm. There can be no distractions, which is why it feels so lonely. You have proven yourself to Me through obedience and by listening to My voice. What I will reveal about upcoming events in your country will be very important. The church will be caught off guard. This is not a revelation for the world, but for My faithful end-time church.

"Children born now will be central in the coming struggle. Few will stay loyal when persecution starts. Few will choose Me. Even now, the spirit of the antichrist is active. But a remnant of My faithful church will remain, and that is who I want you to speak to.

"I will reveal Myself to you, My child. I will provide you with the words and encouragement you need. Support will come, even from unexpected places. Keep going with what you're doing. I understand that the trouble in your life makes it hard to focus, but you will find peace as you follow the purpose I have given you.

"You will begin to see that those close to you are not there by chance but are placed by Me with eternal purpose."

As the Lord speaks, I listen carefully and speak His words aloud to myself. I understand that trusting human systems for salvation rather than God leads to destruction.

"A dark current moves through the minds of leaders, passing from one to another, binding them in a cycle of deception. It does not stop. It grows.

"I see them carried along, no longer in control, yet believing they are. They speak boldly, but their words are empty. They are lifted before the world, displayed, praised, and followed. Yet what is presented as truth is corrupted, shaped by darkness, and will not endure.

"What seems powerful now will vanish. Names of people who appear significant will be forgotten. And in the end, each one will stand alone, with nothing to hold onto, no voice to answer, no escape from what they chose.

"Demonic influence is growing, and darkness will continue to spread. Those who carry My light will face ridicule, mockery, and rejection. What appears to be light will be revealed for what it truly is, but only those led by My Spirit will discern it.

"I created men and women with a purpose, not so they could follow every desire. I came to set them free from sin. Sin cannot remain in My kingdom. I overcame it so that man could enter the light, find freedom in Me, and live in obedience.

"Those lacking faith will struggle. They will know the truth yet still submit to the god of this world. Many raised in the truth will begin to compromise, supporting what they know is wrong to gain acceptance. They will want to seem modern, independent, and different from those who raised them.

"Satan will draw them into what is popular. Because their hearts are being shaped by darkness, they will begin to turn against those who loved them and raised them in truth. There will be rebellion. There will be coldness. But do not give up on the children. Pray. Pray. Pray.

"Many will return to the light in the end. But many will also be lost, not because they were unaware, but because they stopped caring. They will believe the lie that I am no longer relevant."

"Eternity will come quickly. There will be little time to reconsider. The truth they once heard will torment them, echoing long after their choices are made."

"O Father, strengthen those who carry Your light. Let them speak boldly and stand firm. Reveal their calling and grant them courage. Protect them. Grant parents the strength to keep praying. Save souls for Your glory. And help me see what I need to see, even as my heart is breaking."

35

The Path of the False Prophet

As I sat at the table with John and Daniel, my heart broke under the weight of what I had seen, the sorrow of wayward children and the gravity of their choices. Who could have imagined that turning away from loving parents would become so common? God's Word speaks of children becoming disobedient, boastful, and proud, loving only themselves. These are trying times.

Of course, this sets the stage for a ruler, one who will appear godlike in power, speaking great, convincing lies that sound like truth and leading the spiritually blind toward destruction.

"My friends, you both spoke of an end-times Antichrist. I am seeing this now, and it is painful. The weight of it is hard to bear. There is such loneliness and unjust treatment. People love this world and desire a leader who will affirm it and rule in accordance with their desires. They are not concerned with whether it is the one true God.

"They are willing to follow anyone who claims authority and affirms their beliefs. They seek reassurance that everything will be fine and that they will remain in control. That is what they are looking for, and they'll find someone who tells them what they want to hear: that sin doesn't exist, that Jesus wasn't necessary, and that His sacrifice was pointless. They are rejecting the truth."

"Yes, Faustina," John said gently, "it is written, and it must come to pass. But take heart. It will not last forever. Soon, the New Heaven and the New Earth will come, where righteousness dwells."

I found comfort in being with my friends, but I was completely exhausted from the journey. I began to question why I had to do this.

Why did I need to walk these lonely paths and write down what Jesus showed me? It felt pointless.

As soon as those thoughts came, I felt ashamed. Had not Jesus been telling me for years to do exactly this, to be faithful, to pray, to observe, to write, and not to worry about who reads it? In Him, everything is already finished.

Then I heard His lovely voice.

"The words men speak carry power on the Earth. Just as My words do not return empty, neither will the words I give you. They will accomplish what I intend. Do not concern yourself with who will read them or what they will produce. My ways are higher than yours, and My thoughts are beyond your understanding.

"No prophet fully knew what their words would accomplish for future generations. They obeyed Me. I ask you to do the same: come away, listen, write, pray, and release what I give you. This is My instruction to you.

"You are not like others who write, promote, and measure success by numbers. Your calling is different. It is eternal. It may feel hidden and lonely now, but it is not unseen. Heaven is watching.

"I will lift you in the Spirit and reveal what must be known. I will give you words that strengthen My end-time church—words for this time, words from My heart.

"You pray as you write. The words you receive and the visions you have are prayers offered before Me. Not everyone records their prayers, but I am asking you to do so—to keep a record of what I will do and to show that I respond to those who come to Me with a sincere heart.

"Don't worry about what others think of you. You're not writing for them. Your calling didn't come from them. You're writing for Me. The words I give you will reach those they're meant for, even if it's just one person. Just keep going where I have placed you."

"Lord, tell me about fasting. I have fasted much. Why is it important?"

"Fasting is a small act with great impact. Much is accomplished in a short time. I understand your physical needs. I know your heart. I am compassionate. You have shown that you will obey Me, even when it requires sacrifice.

"Also, remember this: mankind will enter its final season when sin and darkness seem to dominate. But it will not last. Satan does not know how much time is left, but he knows it is brief. You seek peace, but for now you will keep walking through a world in conflict until I return to rule and reign.

"Let me speak through you, my child. I know it is hard to let go, to endure loss, and to feel alone. I hear your sadness. A time is coming when the choice between light and darkness will be unavoidable. You cannot hold on to both. Choose wisely, because your choice now shapes what comes next.

"There will be no returning to this moment.

"And yes... he has asked for you."

"Who has?"

"Satan."

"Why?"

"Because you return to Me. Even when you are wounded, you come back. Even when you are tired and sick, you still seek Me. You may struggle and grow weary, but your devotion remains.

"You are a light in the darkness. At times it may seem dim, at times it may burn brightly, but it remains. Your desire to follow Me sets you apart.

"Satan sees this and seeks to pull you away. But no hardship, no pain, will stop you from coming back to Me.

"You are Mine, and I love you."

36

The Path of Righteousness

Faustina was excited when she saw a sign that read, "The Path of Righteousness." At last, an easy road. But she would soon learn it was perhaps the hardest path of all.

The day was just beginning, with the fresh scent of spring and the sound of birdsong. It was beautiful. Faustina felt refreshed and ready to continue her journey. She looked ahead and saw a field of delicate, shimmering red roses.

"That's where I am going?" she exclaimed, excitement rising within her.

John and Daniel had prepared her breakfast: eggs, toast, and strawberries. She had filled her water bottle, packed protein bars, and brought her notebook. She needed to record everything she had seen so she could share it later.

She felt a sense of urgency, afraid of missing this path and somehow ending up on a darker one again. She began to run, but without watching her step, she suddenly stumbled into the dirt.

A knotty branch, hidden beneath the surface, had tripped her.

Pride comes before a fall.

Have I been prideful? I don't think so. I have been faithful. I have endured. Surely that matters. Surely there is something in that worth acknowledging. Others have encouraged me. They have found hope in my words and in my life. Even Jesus said I am wonderful!

Doesn't that mean something?

I have walked a difficult path. I have sacrificed. I have made it this far. I am close to home now. This should be a victory.

Even the enemy fears me.

Suddenly, Faustina felt hungry, though she had just eaten. Then thirst. A strange, unrelenting void was bubbling up inside her. She drank water, but it did nothing. The more she drank, the thirst remained.

A swirl of dust formed nearby, and George appeared, slightly out of breath.

"Hello, Faustina," he said, leaning against a tree.

"George... what are you doing here?"

"I'm here to help."

"Okay..."

"What you are feeling is not hunger for food or thirst for water. You are hungry and thirsty for righteousness. But you cannot receive righteousness while pride remains in your heart. And I should know."

"What are you talking about? I'm the most humble person I know. Everyone says so."

"You know the Lord sees your thoughts."

"Yes..."

"He showed me what you were thinking. Your thoughts were filled with pride about your journey, your endurance, your survival. Yet you know that everything you have done has only been possible because of Him."

"Yes, but I still had to say yes. Doesn't that matter?"

"It does. But even that comes from Him. Even the ability to say yes is given by Him. Remember, our righteousness, on our own, is nothing."

George sat down on a nearby bench.

"I'll stay here," he said calmly. "You walk a little farther and come back if you need to talk."

"Alright..."

So I'm hungry for righteousness? I thought. I assumed I already had it.

Suddenly, the sky darkened. Raindrops pelted me. Wind rose out of nowhere, fierce and violent, lifting dead leaves into spiraling bursts.

I'm trying to do what is right... so why is this so hard? Why does pride rise so quickly in me, even when I try to do good? I've lost so much. I've given up everything. And still... this?

Phantoms with large yellow eyes began to emerge from the storm, pressing into her thoughts. A deep despair overwhelmed her, a crushing sense of worthlessness, and a question of why she even existed.

She tried to run, but the wind tore at her. Her notebook got soaked. Her water bottle slipped from her hand into the mud. When she reached for it, she fell forward into the puddle, sinking into it much more deeply than seemed possible.

"George? Where are you?"

She thought she heard his voice, "I'm right here", but she wasn't certain.

She forced herself onto her hands and knees and crawled back the way she came, searching for him.

"What happened?" she gasped. "I was fine, and then suddenly everything changed."

"What you experienced," George said, "is how quickly pride can destroy a soul. Even when good is done, man begins to believe he can become righteous through his own efforts. But all righteousness comes from the Lord. Without Him, we can do nothing. I know this well.

"Man is quick to take credit for what God has done through him. He forgets that it is God who gives strength, wisdom, and ability. Without Him, we are drawn toward darkness.

“Even in doing good, the question remains: do we truly know Him? Or are we only doing things in His name while our hearts remain distant?

We must trust Him for salvation, not ourselves.”

“Be thankful that darkness came so quickly. That is what pride does: it darkens the soul. It makes us believe we can earn salvation through our own goodness. But that is not the truth.

“The good news is this: you can return to Him. Confess. Lay everything at His feet. Acknowledge that without Him, you are nothing, but with Him, all things are possible.

“You experienced only a moment of darkness. The unredeemed will experience it forever.”

He paused.

“And you will also encounter envy. People will envy you, your voice, your presence, your life. That is the nature of man. Learn how to respond when it comes.”

“Can I sit down?”

“Of course.”

I sat down on the grass, trembling, overwhelmed by what I had just experienced.

“I don’t know what to do.”

“Stay here,” he said. “Pray. The Lord will show you.”

He handed me a rose.

“For you.”

“Thank you...”

I lifted it to my nose and breathed in its healing fragrance as the soft petals kissed my cheek.

Then suddenly, an incredible feeling of love came over me.

I dropped it instantly, surprised by what I was experiencing.

Afraid he read my thoughts, I looked around for George, but he was gone.

As I sought the Lord, I drifted into a deep, tender sleep, dreaming of loving a man I had never truly known in this way. We were united spiritually in a way that felt both foreign and profoundly intimate. A luminous presence of the Holy Spirit hovered above us, binding our souls in a sacred dance. I felt a subtle ache, wondering whether this was a new temptation to resist or a yearning to embrace with all my heart. And dare I speak of the man in my dream?

Why now, with so many paths still ahead, does this longing feel so urgent, so real? And why does the loss of it feel so profound?

So much for thinking I was on an easy path.

Through many trials... we enter the Kingdom of God.

36

Path of Dishonest Politicians and Media Figures

A path built on lies stretched out before me. How can I describe what it looked like? It seemed harmless and well-traveled, yet at its entrance lay a dark tunnel, like a wind pulling people in. They moved with urgency, as if racing toward something they believed they could not afford to miss.

To see this path for what it truly is, you must recognize the truth. Influential voices in politics and media spread falsehoods quickly, shaping the minds of those who do not question what they hear. To those who do not know the truth, their words sound convincing, even trustworthy.

As soon as I noticed the tunnel, I was pulled into it and suddenly found myself in a small, brightly lit room. I wondered if I was about to be part of a performance. I sat at a table while makeup was applied to my face. Several wigs rested on stands before me. A hurried beautician approached, tucked my hair into a net, and placed a wig on my head. It matched my hair color, just styled differently. Perfect.

I could get used to this.

"Faustina, we have breaking news you need to be briefed on. Come to the studio quickly," an important-looking man said. He was attractive, but there was something in his presence that unsettled me. I forced a polite smile.

What am I doing?

It became clear this was not a play. It was a news station. Everything felt staged, controlled, polished. People moved quickly, dressed sharply, speaking with confidence.

George would love this.

And then he was there, handing me a bottle of water and slices of lemon.

"Hello, George."

"Faustina, we don't know each other here. Keep your voice down."

"Okay. That feels strange."

"It has a purpose. I'll be here when you're done. I'll show you how to leave."

"Is it really that complicated?"

"Yes. This place is spiritually dark and seductive. The man you spoke to has been watching you. He has offered you a promotion in exchange for something."

"What do you mean?"

"He expects you to sleep with him."

"What? Absolutely not."

"That's how things work here. If you want to be promoted, you give something in return."

"That's wrong. I want to leave now."

"Not yet. The Lord wants you to understand what people here face. To feel it. To see it. So you can respond with compassion, not judgment."

He paused, then looked at me differently.

"You look... very striking."

I blushed, feeling embarrassed at his attention.

"Five minutes, Faustina!" someone called out.

I felt uneasy after meeting the director. He explained that the information I was supposed to present wasn't entirely truthful, but that it would boost ratings. He urged me to bend the truth and present it convincingly.

Then he handed me a key to a hotel room and suggested we meet there after the broadcast.

I hesitated.

He quickly added that a promotion was likely, since I was under consideration.

Soon after, I was led into the studio and seated under dim lighting.

"Two minutes to air. Ten seconds. Three... two... one."

The director pointed toward the camera. Bright lights penetrated.

"Good evening, I'm Faustina..."

"George?" I called out quietly after I did what I had to do on the set.

The broadcast went smoothly, but it felt empty. Artificial. I spoke words I knew were not true. Images appeared on screen that had been manipulated or created.

Is this how it works?

I felt dizzy. Disoriented.

And now I was expected to meet my boss at a hotel.

"George? How do I leave this place?"

"My child, do not be afraid. It is I."

The Lord's voice reached me.

"Lord, forgive me. I spoke what was not true. And now..."

"You have a way out but take this truth with you. Many are trapped in this cycle, chasing success and trading truth for gain. Pray for them. Some will still turn to Me. Show compassion. I died for them as well."

"Yes, Lord. I will. Please help me leave."

I heard movement and turned. George was crouched low in the bushes by the window of my dressing room.

"Come. This way."

He led me out through the window and onto the street below. Neon lights flashed all around us. The city felt alive and overwhelming.

We took a cab and arrived at the airport.

"Where are we going?" I asked.

"I'm not sure," George replied, smiling. "But isn't this exciting?"

He took my hand, and suddenly everything was well again.

38

The False Path of the Rapture

I saw a world overwhelmed by fiery chaos and a false path meant to lead them out. Not a literal fire, but a deep, spreading turmoil of suffering and heartbreak that touched every life. Some endured physical pain, while others were emotionally shattered.

Children turned away from their parents in need, deceived and led into false beliefs. Many abandoned the elderly, placing them in care homes and visiting them rarely, if at all. Some cut ties completely because their family held to traditional values and followed Scripture, which the children dismissed as man-made.

They surrounded themselves with voices that reshaped truth, selecting only what suited them while ignoring what challenged them. They created a version of God that reflected their own desires and rejected those who remained faithful to Him.

The mother who gave them life was now seen as burdensome and unnecessary. Love had grown cold in many hearts. I struggled to understand it.

My mother was not perfect, but she was my mother, and I loved her. She chose life and received what God had given. Yet many now reject that same gift, claiming complete authority over their bodies, even when new life exists within them. There is a painful contradiction in this. People claim ownership of something temporary, yet one day they will leave it behind. If they refuse to trust the Lord, both body and soul will face judgment.

Some parents continue to pray, fast, and believe for their children to return. Others draw closer to God in their grief, trusting what Scripture has already warned. But many become overwhelmed and begin listening only to voices that promise escape.

They are told that everything will soon end, that they will be removed before suffering comes. Because of this, they stop preparing. They stop growing. They begin to live for comfort, for prosperity, for the pleasures of this world.

They convince themselves that their choices no longer matter. They search Scripture not to understand truth, but to confirm what they already believe.

Many leaders promote this message, and it spreads easily because it appeals to desire. It promises ease, success, and blessing without surrender. But it leads to destruction.

You can't hold onto this world and belong completely to the Lord at the same time. One will always pull you away from the other.

An evil ruler will rise and highly regard this false path. He will deceive many who believe they are secure. When hardship comes, their faith will collapse. They will begin to doubt everything. Some will turn away completely.

This path is dangerous. It must be recognized for what it is before it is too late.

Many who claim faith live without reverence, treating grace as something to be used rather than honored. Gatherings grow, but often because of personality, influence, and financial appeal.

People give freely, hoping to secure their future, while avoiding the deeper call to transformation.

Leaders who speak this way often hear only themselves, even when they believe they are hearing God. Their message is shaped by desire, not truth. It spreads because it is welcomed.

I found myself sitting in one of these gatherings. A soft fragrance filled the air. When I lifted my wrist, I realized it was my perfume.

I glanced at the man beside me and wondered if he noticed. He was striking, calm, his eyes closed as the prayer began.

Then I looked closer.

It was George.

"George," I whispered.

"Quiet," he replied softly.

I almost laughed. I should be used to this by now. I settled into my seat, preparing to listen. But the message was filled with false assurance. It was difficult to remain silent.

The Lord spoke to me.

"Speak, My child. Find those who are still faithful, even if they are hidden. Tell them that tribulation is not abandonment. I am refining My people. They are being prepared.

"Suffering does not mean I love them less. It is part of the work I am doing in them. Tell them to return to Scripture. Tell them to seek truth, not the comfort of false voices. Go to them."

I listened, taking it in, then glanced at George.

He seemed completely absorbed in the message. Later, he said it was one of the most powerful teachings he had heard, especially regarding the claim that believers would not suffer, even though the truth is that the true Church would suffer greatly.

George took my hand firmly and led me quickly out of the building. People stared at us. George said it was because we were so beautiful. I laughed, thinking he was mostly joking. I did not feel beautiful, but tired and old.

A sharp pain pressed behind my eyes.

"Lord... help me."

I passed out in George's arms and woke up on the beach. George said he had superpowers from God and could take me anywhere. I happily began to believe him.

39

The Liars Path

Many walk a false path. Deceived souls reject God, curse Him, and turn away from His ways, yet refuse to change. They claim to represent Jesus but do not truly know Him. They shape Him in their own image, but He is nothing like them.

They say they will pray when tragedy strikes, but their hearts remain unrepentant. They persist in their ways, and their prayers show no surrender. "The Liars Path" is crowded with souls, yet few see the danger.

They live in sin without realizing it because their vision is clouded. Still, they believe they are good. They assume Jesus is pleased with them because they support worthy causes, yet they don't see that the brokenness they oppose is rooted in the very sin they accept. They are heading toward destruction without realizing it.

I found myself once again at a church service, alone. The pastor wore a rainbow sash and read from a version of Scripture I did not recognize. It sounded more like a paraphrase than the truth of God's word. Around me, people moved in unsettling ways. Some were dressed in ways that blurred identity, performing more like a display than worship. The congregation swayed as if caught in something they did not fully understand yet were captive to.

I wanted to stand and read from my Bible, but I could not move. It felt as if a weight were pressing down on me. I tried to shift, but my body would not respond.

Suddenly, the service ended, and everyone walked outside together. We gathered in the parking lot, heading toward different cars. I tried to leave, but someone insisted I go with them.

I hesitated, but before I could refuse, I found myself in the car.

A large sign with bold red paint was placed in my hands.

"MY BODY! MY CHOICE! NO UTERUS? NO OPINION!"

I froze.

We were heading to a rally.

When we arrived, another group was already there. Tension filled the air immediately. The woman driving, Tish, began shouting. She threw her water bottle at a poster that showed stages of a child's development.

What am I doing here, Lord? I do not belong here. Please, get me out.

Then suddenly, everything shifted.

Tish began to cry.

I did not know what to do.

"Why did you come today?" she asked me.

"I don't know," I said quietly.

"Will you pray for me?"

"Yes."

I began to pray.

And in that moment, something changed.

Tish said she saw Jesus. She said He told her that He loved her. She began to weep, saying she was sorry for the life she had been living. She wanted to be free. She wanted to become who God had created her to be.

I held her as she cried and agreed with her prayer.

A young girl, about 16, came up to me when the prayer ended and asked if she could talk to me. She told me she didn't want to kill her baby, but she had nowhere to go because her parents had kicked her out of the house. I prayed with her, and suddenly a kind woman appeared and offered her everything she needed, including a place to stay and medical care for her and her baby. The girl cried, gave me a quick hug of gratitude, and was off. As she walked away, she asked me my name and said she'd name her baby after me if she had a girl. What a joy it was!

Then, just as suddenly as it began, it was over.

And I found myself once again on the path, unsure where it would lead next.

40

The Path of Sin out of Eden

I did not want to be on this path at all. I can only imagine how awful it was when our ancestors committed the original sin. I needed to talk with John and Daniel before moving forward. I already carried enough weight from my own family, and trying to trace everything back to the beginning felt overwhelming. Maybe they could help me understand.

"Hello, brothers," I called at the entrance to the cave. "I'm back."

"Sister Faustina, come in and sit! We've missed you," John said, his eyes filled with warmth.

"I've missed you, too. The journey has been... a lot. The Lord has taken me through so many paths."

"There is something we need to give you," John said. "A letter came for you last week. We did not open it, but we sensed its importance. Daniel, please bring it."

"A letter for me?"

Faustina took the letter and sat by the fire. Daniel brought her tea and oatmeal cookies. She looked at the handwriting. It was from home. From her daughter.

Hello Mother,

We regret to inform you that Father passed away last night. He never regained consciousness after he fell from a ladder. The doctor was unsure of the exact cause but believed it may have been related to alcohol that caused him to fall. He had been drinking heavily. As you know, he often refused medical care.

We do not know if you will receive this, but know that no service has been scheduled. Whether you return or not does not matter to us, as we have told you many times before. We are very busy.

Your Daughters,

Sara and Gracie

Faustina turned the page, expecting more, but there was nothing.

After all this time... nothing more?

She showed the letter to John and Daniel. They grieved with her as she explained how she had written, sent gifts, and tried to stay connected.

"I don't know what I feel about his death," she said quietly. "He hurt me. He did not love me well. But I never wished him dead. I hope he found the Lord before the end."

She was to remain with them for several days, listening, asking questions, trying to understand what lay ahead. Though her heart wept anew, she was determined to carry on the Lord's work.

Faustina spoke of the next path her Lord was leading her to—the "Path of Sin out of Eden". Sin had changed everything. It had redirected humanity's course, yet God had already made a way from the beginning. Even before the fall, there had been a plan. Through Jesus, the second Adam, a new covenant was established. Still, many would not choose the path Jesus's coming opened to all. They would follow the road that began in Eden and led to eternal destruction, ignoring the signs pointing toward life. With so much temptation to return to the ease of Eden, can God really blame us for wanting comfort here on Earth, even if that comfort could no longer be found? She felt as though she were in limbo—not able to go back to Eden, yet uncertain of the way forward, or even whether one existed.

"How can anyone stay on the right path? Things on Earth are so devastatingly hard! Can God blame us for simply yearning to go back to Eden before the fall?" she asked.

"It is only through Jesus," John said. "He has made the way. If we follow Him and hold to His words, we will arrive safely in the restored Eden. No one can go back and redo the beginning. "

"Pride leads man to believe he can find another way," Daniel added. "Some even believe they can fight against God's plan. Deception leads them there. In the end, truth remains.

"The path away from Eden once felt powerful and freeing. Humanity didn't realize what was lost when walking close to God. Creation was full of beauty and order. Sin distorted everything.

"A new Heaven and a new Earth are coming, where everything will be restored. What is now called freedom will be revealed as bondage, and what is called restriction by following the Lord will be revealed as true freedom."

"God...must I?" I asked, fear rising within me as my view widened.

One moment I had been with John and Daniel, and the next I stood on broken stones beneath a darkening sky.

"Come. Follow My voice. The light is ahead. Darkness is falling, but you will reach it if you keep your eyes on Me."

I reached out and felt a hand beside me. It was George.

"Oh... you're here too?"

"Yes," he said with trepidation. "It feels like the moment when Adam and Eve left the garden. I'll be Adam, and you can be Eve."

I let out a small laugh, hesitant about whether this was a role I ever wanted to play. We found ourselves in the garden, more breathtaking than anything I had ever seen. The greenery was vibrant and energetic, the air was filled with the scent of life, and the birds serenaded us beneath a sky so brilliantly blue it seemed freshly created. But suddenly we were moving forward.

"Why are we leaving?" I whispered. "This is unbearable."

The beauty began to fade. Sounds died down, then shifted. The world felt unfamiliar.

"The innocence is gone," George said. "Sin has changed everything. It will not be restored until God makes all things new."

"This is too much," I said. "What are we supposed to do?"

"Keep walking," the Lord's gentle voice encouraged us. "Your journey is moving you forward. No life is without purpose, even amid the heavy burden of sin now running through your veins. You are called to know Me and walk with Me. Many will choose the easy, temporary path, allowing sin to rule them, but it leads to destruction. Stay faithful. Continue. Even when it does not make sense, I am with you."

A great eagle passed overhead, its appearance unsettling. I saw animals fleeing, their movements frantic and confused. The world felt as though it was unraveling. Darkness filled the air.

The air became heavy. Breathing grew difficult. Everything felt corrupted. "Jesus... where are You?"

"Faustina, this is the path sin has created for humanity. When suffering comes, many blame Me, yet few thank Me for what I have given. Even in a fallen world, there is still provision, still purpose. Death will come to all, but there is still hope beyond it. I grieve for those who reject that hope."

I looked at my hands. They had aged. Wrinkled. Weak.

"George... we are getting old."

"Yes," he said quietly.

"We are fading. There is no stopping it."

"This is only a glimpse," he replied. "It shows what was lost and what remains until all is made new."

Pain spread through my body. My strength was leaving me.

"I can't keep going," I whispered.

The world fell silent. No sound. No movement.

It felt as though everything was coming to a sudden end.

We lay on the ground, holding onto each other as the world around us faded. I closed my eyes, surrendering to what I thought was death.

Then suddenly, I felt his hand release mine as sin separated us.

A multicolored serpent with a large head slithered across me, its eyes glowing, its presence cold. It struck, yet I felt no pain.

A large angel stood nearby, radiant. He quickly flung the snake from me.

Unexpectedly, I heard a cart being pushed across the floor.

I opened my eyes.

A sterile room. White walls.

An elderly man sat nearby, struggling to eat. Across from him, an elderly woman lay in bed, her breathing uneven, her hands curled around a tissue.

"We are here now... my love," the man whispered.

"My love?" she replied weakly. "When did that happen?"

"I don't remember," he said softly.

"It is sad... being this old," she murmured before coughing.

"Yes. But not for long," he said. "Soon we will go to our eternal home."

"George?"

"Yeah."

"In case we die, I just want you to know...... I love you."

George responded with a loud snore as he drifted off to sleep.

41

The Path of the Loss of the Body

From what I overheard in a conversation between the doctor and the nurse, I realized I had been living in a nursing home for five years. The atmosphere in my solitary, dimly lit room felt bleak. There were no visitors, no voices of loved ones, only silence. I was mostly immobile. Tears streamed down my face as I mourned my loneliness. Sometimes I thought I heard George speak, but now I am unsure whether I truly did or simply wanted to hear his voice.

I was wheeled into a smaller, darker room next to mine. My short white hair was matted, and my robe hung loosely around me. In my deep sense of forsakenness, I called out to Jesus in desperation, and instantly I felt His gentle hand rest on my shoulder. When I looked up, I saw an angel. He was hidden from others yet visible to me, blending into the wall's whiteness. He was massive and awe-inspiring. His presence radiated power, faith, and hope. His stillness was profound, yet his eyes burned with divine fire. I cherished his presence until I fell asleep.

Then I heard voices, familiar voices. Someone entered the room. It was my late husband. He looked around and saw only a bed with drawn curtains, missing me in the dark space beside it. Confused, he left without realizing I was there. Another family member looked in from the hallway and saw only an empty bed. She couldn't find me either, and I couldn't tell what she felt. Suddenly, I heard George again. He had aged a lot. He called my name, and in that moment, he seemed to realize I was in that shadowed room, even though the door was closed.

He called out, "I know where you are, but He won't let me enter."

Then Jesus nodded to the angel. With a single motion, He signaled that it was time. The angel reached out and lifted me away. In that moment, I was young again, dressed in white with long, flowing hair. I felt at peace, filled with joy, able to speak, completely renewed, and embraced by eternal love. I was going home.

Heaven at last! I bathed in the soft glow, feeling my body unshackled as my senses awakened with joy. Suddenly, overwhelming regret pulled me back to reality. The desire to remain in that divine realm flooded me. I longed to return home, away from this earthly existence, into the embrace of eternal love.

My beloved Jesus spoke softly to me with gentleness and grace. "Faustina, let's go for a walk."

Hand in hand, we walked until we found a bench, then sat together, taking in the beauty around us. I breathed deeply and smelled the sweetest roses. They hung above my head, stretching endlessly along the path, across the fields, and through the trees. Their fragrance and beauty filled my heart with awe. I felt Jesus's presence in the roses, as if His love whispered through their petals. Gratitude welled up within me.

I thought of George. He often carried roses. How could he know exactly where I was without searching? How did he sense my presence in that hidden room, unseen by others? Was there something deeper between us, beyond friendship? The thought both excited and unsettled me. I tried not to dwell on it, but the connection felt undeniable. I knew he had been acting differently lately, but everything about this journey had been strange. It seemed natural that he would be affected too. Stress can change a person. It can make them act strangely, even sickly.

I knew my devotion to Jesus was unwavering. I belonged to Him completely. Still, in quiet moments, I found myself wishing I had lived longer. I wanted more time with George, to understand what had grown between us and whether it was truly love. My heart felt torn, divided between divine love and the quiet pull of human affection. I feared I might be mistaken. Memories surfaced of times when I longed for love that was never returned. I also remembered those who felt the same about me, and I could not return their feelings. It is strange how we remember the pain we received more clearly than the pain we caused. My answer to this struggle was simple. I prayed. Again.

"Jesus, please, to prevent any more pain or embarrassment, take George out of my life."

The Lord answered quickly. I saw George frozen in time. He stood in the exact place where I had last heard him say he knew where I was but could not enter. His body was completely still. He wore an old country shirt. His hair and beard were long and white. A cane stood nearby.

"Alright, keep him there, Lord. I truly do not know what to ask."

I, however, was young again and free. I was grateful that old age had been delayed, at least for now. It seemed I was meant to walk the next part of this path alone. I remembered dying and being carried home to Heaven by an angel. Now I was back, young once more.

Suddenly, I found myself standing outside the nursing home where I had died. I stood on the sidewalk, watching the elderly come and go, some pushed in wheelchairs, others moving slowly with walkers. A few seemed content, but most looked confused or sad.

"What am I doing here, Lord?"

"Go to George."

"George? He is still here?"

"Yes."

I moved quickly through the doors, which opened for me even though they were secured with a code. I found him in my old room. My bed was made, and the room was clean. The smaller room I had shared with Jesus and the angel was gone, if it had ever existed in the physical world.

George stood in the same place where I had last heard him speak.

"George? George?"

"Yes." He stirred and smiled. "I just took a little nap."

"Yeah, that is what old people say. Come on. You are coming with me now."

"Look at you. You are young again."

I glanced at my reflection in the mirror and nodded.

"And you too, George. But please take this tissue. You've been drooling," I said with a laugh.

He saw himself and smiled.

"Oh yes, I am back! Look at my hair," he said with childlike wonder.

Jesus appeared. "The road ahead will be very difficult. There are still battles to fight. Keep your eyes on Me."

"Did you hear that, George?"

Suddenly, the ground beneath us gave way, and we fell, falling for what felt like forever, until we landed in a dark pit. A faint light glowed far above us.

"George, what happened?"

"It seems we have fallen into a pit."

"Yes, I see that. I must get out. I cannot breathe."

"George, are you wearing cologne?"

"No. Why?"

"I cannot breathe. I smell something like incense. I wish I had my inhaler."

"Try to take slow breaths."

"I cannot. Look at these walls. There is no way to climb them. Jesus, help! Get us out of here!"

I closed my eyes, and suddenly I saw Jesus sitting with George on the sofa of a small oceanfront cottage. The scene was beautiful. The walls were lined with windows that framed the roaring sea. Waves crashed against rocks while seagulls cried overhead. The air felt clean and full of warmth. This was my dream.

But why was George there?

For years, I imagined a simple life by the ocean—a white dress, a quiet home, lace curtains fluttering in the breeze. Everything inside was white and peaceful. I felt truly alive there, sitting on the sofa, laughing softly, as if I had rediscovered a happiness I once lost. I prayed that this feeling would last and that the sadness would fade away.

Jesus sat across from me as we talked at the kitchen table, watching me gently.

"I want you to fully surrender to Me," He said. "Then you will have the ability to discern clearly. You are lacking in this, and I allowed this test to strengthen you."

Hope rose in me, but I still resisted. Had I not surrendered before? I felt restless, as though I needed to escape, but I could not go far before returning inside.

And George.

He was walking along the beach, talking with beautiful women, his confidence relaxed and natural. He smiled, laughed, and kept close to them. His eyes lingered. He softly asked if he could pray with them. Some were surprised. Some leaned in closer, attracted to him. He resisted some advances, but not all. A few prayed with him. Others moved closer, their proximity turning into something more before he gently pulled away.

"I am sorry if you thought that was my intention," he said quietly, a faint smile on his lips.

Even as he spoke with them, he kept glancing back toward the house where I was with Jesus. When he returned, he acted as though nothing had happened.

I did not know if this was who he truly was.

Then jealousy rose in me, sudden and overwhelming.

I did not understand what I was seeing.

Pain and anger settled in my chest. I looked out again and saw a woman on the beach, flawless, radiant. George kissed her deeply, and they fell together into the sand.

I stood there, watching.

Then Jesus stepped in front of the window. "Faustina. Come away from the window. What you saw was not real."

I began to pray, trying to understand why I was being shown all of this. I remembered that house. I had seen it many times before. In those memories, I was alone. I lived there alone. I died there alone.

Now I was there again.

But this time, I was not alone.

The darkness engulfed me completely. Great cement walls seemed to close in, suffocating and relentless. My breathing grew shallow, almost ceasing altogether. I lost consciousness to the tumult of crashing waves and the absolute solitude, as waves of reflection and terror surged within me, leaving me powerless to escape.

42

The Path of Heart's Desire

I met a man today, the most beautiful man I have ever known. I encountered him unexpectedly. I was standing at an intersection, contemplating which path God would have me take and what He wanted to teach me. My mind was still troubled by having survived after coming so close to death. But I understand now that when we die on Earth, we do not truly die in eternity. God performs miracles, and the resurrection of the body into glorious eternal life is one of the most incredible miracles we will ever witness. I am a miracle.

We catch glimpses of eternity here on Earth. We cannot always know whether someone we pray for can hear us, because the spirit remains alive and receptive even as the physical body weakens or the mind fades. By God's power, they can still be reached, come to know Jesus, and pass through Heaven's eternal gates.

I walked away feeling young again. I was an old woman who died and came back to life.

So, back to this man. His eyes held a hazel glow, green and brown like my mother's. His hair was long and wavy, and when he smiled, I truly caught my breath. He seemed to know me, and I knew him.

He said hello, and I replied, aware that there were countless other things I wanted to say, more than a lifetime could hold. I wanted to leave with him and talk forever, but even that would not be enough. He stood beside a tree blooming with delicate white flowers. The scent was heavenly, the kind you would want to carry with you and keep close.

I loved this man, and I knew he loved me. I thought this must be how it feels when you meet the person you are meant to spend your life with.

A quiet understanding. A connection that exists even without words. I leaned against the tree beside him and breathed. He laughed, as if he understood me completely.

Then he asked if I wanted to walk by the river. I could hear the nearby water flowing gently. Of course, I said yes.

We walked and talked, and then we walked some more. It was beautiful. I realized I had forgotten to eat. I had forgotten what hunger felt like. I had forgotten everything else.

At the end of our walk, Jesus was there.

Immediately, I felt torn. I did not sense that He was unhappy with me, but I knew He wanted to tell me something.

"What is it, my Lord? Who is this man?" I asked, though I knew.

"My child, when I walked on Earth, many women loved Me, and I loved them too. But I did not form a union with any of them, because My calling from the Father was greater. I want you to understand what it means to desire someone and not be able to be with them."

"I do not understand. Do you not bring people together? If two people feel this way, should they not come together and share their lives?"

"Yes, I do. But sometimes there are reasons that prevent that union. It may be that someone did not trust Me and chose another, and now they are committed to the vow they made. Then meeting the one they were meant for brings both great joy and deep pain."

"Oh, my Father. I do not want to be tormented like this. Please take these feelings away. Please show me how to surrender him to You and lay him on the altar before You. Or better yet, show me how to walk away so completely that he becomes like something I will never have to face again."

Jesus laughed softly. "Yes, that would be easier. But I want you to trust Me. Trust Me with these feelings. Trust Me with the future you cannot see. Some believe I am a God who always says no, but that is not who I am. I desire to fulfill the dreams of My children's hearts. I desire to do so in a way that brings lasting blessing, a gift that will bring joy to many in the years to come. Trust Me. Right now, it may feel like bondage, but that can change, even if these feelings seem stronger than anything you have ever known. Let Me walk through this with you. I created love. I am love. I am working beyond what you can see. I am eternal, and you are eternal. Do not despair. I am the author of love. Let Me come to you in a new way and be your husband."

Then Jesus was gone, and I was left with the man again.

It felt like a strange temptation because I knew we weren't meant to be together right now. I sensed the Lord had lessons for me, things He wanted to reveal, and experiences I needed to go through to understand His heart better. But I was able to walk away because My Lord was calling.

43

The Path of Romance

Suddenly, I found myself on the beach. It was beautiful, with crystal-clear water that felt refreshing. Sea creatures surrounded me, and I lost myself in the joy of watching them through my snorkel mask. The visibility was incredible, as if the sea itself were illuminated. I moved freely in and out of the water, without fear. No creatures there could harm me. I knew the shore was close, and Jesus was there, waiting for me so we could walk along the sand and ride horses by the water. Later, there would be fish to enjoy around a campfire. Just me and Jesus, forever. Love without end.

I felt beautiful, and I knew I was. My long hair fell in soft waves down my back as I held close in my heart the One who had shown me, in the most undeniable way, how deeply He loves me.

Near where I stood, the water was divided. One side was pure, where I remained, and the other was dark and corrupted. Jesus held back the dark side to protect me, just as He parted the Red Sea. The water beside me was black and thick, like oil. A man stood there with his head above the surface, wearing a foolish expression. He claimed he was safe because his head was above the water, but that was not true. He was dying.

Beneath that dark surface lay dangerous creatures, demons, and the burden of sin. Everything he had committed himself to over the years was there, including the things he once loved, the entertainment he embraced, and the places where darkness reigned. He saw no problem with his life because those around him lived the same way. He criticized me, saying I spent too much time in the light and that I was rigid and self-righteous. But darkness and light cannot coexist.

Then I understood. The man was my former husband. He had been given many chances to come into the light, but he refused. He chose darkness. He tried to pull me into it with him, but I would not go. Now he stood there alone, convinced that I was the one with the problem because I chose to stay where I was.

Many people give themselves over to darkness for the sake of recognition on Earth, only to discover too late that they are trapped in something they cannot escape. But God called me into the light, and I answered.

Soon, the dark water and the man would be gone. He was meant to be a gift from the Lord to me—someone who would stand with me, pray with me, strengthen me, and share in what God was doing. But he did not walk in that calling, and that is why he was taken.

Still, I sensed there was more ahead. I knew I was not to fear the future. God was in control, and I would not be alone.

I sat in a chair on the beach, taking in the day, when I saw George. I could tell by the way he walked toward me that something had changed. Not in his appearance, but within him.

"George, how are you? Where have you been?"

"Here and there. How do I look?"

"You look good. What is going on?"

"I have been in many battles in which I barely escaped."

"What or whom were you fighting?"

"The enemies of our soul, without a doubt. My horse, Goldie, suffered severe wounds when she charged into a tangle of barbed wire, but the Lord healed her completely. The accuser of the brethren dragged me into desolate, shadowy places, yet I was clad in the armor of God. Nonetheless, the battle was fierce. I found myself overwhelmed, even despairing of life itself!"

"Really? Tell me more."

"I was trying to take a nap when this incredibly gorgeous woman woke me by rubbing my back. It felt wonderful, and before I knew it, she was trying to reach other parts of my body. I felt powerless to stop her. I wasn't sure if I was sleeping or if this was real. I called on Jesus, and He appeared before me in the clouds, telling me to rise and walk towards the water.

"I managed to get to my feet, and in that moment, she staggered backward. Guilt gnawed at me—had I hurt her? Instinctively, I reached out to help, but her hand was black and twisted. I quickly withdrew my hand and ran, but suddenly she was the stunning woman again, flanked by three others—tall, blond, and almost ethereal. One of them called out to me, asking if I knew a verse about a woman's virtues. I love to share scripture, but at that instant, I remembered—we are called to flee temptation.

"I recognized it as a trap, so I kept heading toward the water and jumped in. My head banged into the sand because the water was suddenly too shallow to swim. Then an angle showed up and pulled me here," George said, pulling seaweed from his wet, tousled hair.

"Were you wearing your armor?"

"That's the odd thing. I thought I was, but I remembered that I took it off to lie on the beach, thinking it would be okay since it felt so safe and comfortable."

"From what I recall, John and Daniel told me, and I know from the Bible, we are tempted by all the temptations common to man. And we all have times when we let our guard down. Tell me, did you recognize those women?"

"Yes! One was from the cruise ship we were on! She looked like my type, but she was not the one for me."

"Sounds like a classic temptation from Satan. Tempting us with things and people that he knows we love.

How is Goldie?"

"She's better. Healing up. Just a little shy now, but she'll be okay."

"I wanted to ask you something. Do you remember what you called me in the nursing home?"

"No. What?"

"Never mind. If you don't remember, then that's okay.

"I am waiting to meet with Jesus."

"Oh. Then tell Him I said hello!"

And then he hopped on Goldie and trotted down the beach.

I stood there, stunned.

What had just happened? Weren't we still talking?

The weight of it settled deep inside me, bringing a sorrow I couldn't put into words. I saw clearly that no matter how hard I tried, I was never truly someone he could choose. I was always on the outside, watching others take the place I could never reach. But then why did I still want him? Am I that weak and needy? Why do I still listen to him?

I do not know why it mattered so much in that moment. Or perhaps it had always mattered, and I had only just now allowed myself to see it.

My appearance had been a struggle my entire life. No matter what I did, I could not become what any man seemed to want. I was unplanned. Unwanted. And that shaped everything.

So why did it matter who I loved?

I had never truly known that kind of love in return.

I now realize that being born into a family doesn't guarantee love from parents or siblings, no matter how much you want it. Having children doesn't ensure they will love or care for you. Marriage doesn't guarantee your husband's loyalty.

Is it love when a man shares himself with someone else just days after committing to you? Is that love from God? He said he loved me, yet he stayed with another woman even after we were married.

I believed him.

Jesus, help me.

Was that really George who was just here? Or was it someone shaped by how I see myself?

I noticed that the sand left no evidence that George and Goldie were even here. That unsettled me.

I felt confused, and more than that, I felt alone.

I wanted someone to take care of me.

Tears streamed down my face as I sat there, watching the sun sink into the sky. Regret filled my mind. Times I didn't trust God. Times I rushed ahead. It seemed to explain why I was alone now, because of the choices I had made.

Was this the result?

No one beside me?

Still, I knew the Lord was with me. He always would be.

The truth is, I loved George more than I could ever explain. I have loved him for a long time.

But who is he, really?

If I must, I will carry this love quietly for the rest of my life, even if it means living with that longing.

There is some comfort in knowing this body will not be needed forever.

I will finish what I was sent here to do. I will walk every path the Lord has set before me. And when that is done, I will go home.

I choose to trust God until the very end.

He brought me here. He redeemed me. And when the time is right, He will take me home.

44

Drunk in the Water

I was sitting on the beach with Jesus, relaxed in a comfortable chair beside Him. He leaned in gently and suggested we step away for a little while. When I turned, I saw the peaceful ocean house I had seen many times before. I thought back to the moments inside, when George and Jesus sat together on the couch while I stayed in the kitchen, unsure of what to do.

Jesus explained that my only task was to remain at peace and continue along the path He had set before me. This unexpected turn in what felt like a wandering journey would eventually lead me to a place of calm and stability. I smiled at my horse, tethered to a post on the beach, grateful for the Lord's blessing of her here at this time.

"Do not worry, my child. I will never abandon you or forsake you. My hand is guiding you, supporting you from before, behind, and above. My presence rests upon you, and My words are in your mouth. You will hear a voice behind you, guiding you on the path you should take, so you will never be alone. Do not be afraid."

How I longed to do that. But my heart felt divided. I wanted what any woman desires. Love from a man. Children. A home. Yet it continued to slip away from me.

Still clinging to that fragile sense of comfort, I dove into the water, swimming as if my life depended on it. The water around me was fiercely bright, like a powerful beam cutting through the deep darkness. Ahead of me lay a vast dividing line, separating me from what lay beyond. In the distance, shadows moved. Demons stretched their hands toward me, reaching, waiting, trying to pull me into the darkness.

My family stood nearby, still and unmoving, as if frozen in place. My husband, who had once died and now appeared again, watched me with a twisted smile. My siblings looked on with contempt, believing I deserved what was happening to me because I spoke openly against things they supported. I defended what I believed was right, but their hostility only grew stronger. They spoke under their breath, laughed, and treated me as if I were nothing.

More figures emerged from the shadows. Members of my own family who completely rejected me. They looked at me with disgust, saying I did not resemble them, that I was too different to belong.

My daughters stood nearby, silent. Their eyes were empty, without warmth or recognition. It was as if I did not exist to them.

"Faustina," Jesus's voice broke through the darkness. "If you say the darkness will fall, then both light and darkness are the same to Me."

He stood between me and the reaching darkness.

"Keep your eyes on Me, my child. This will pass. You will be strengthened because you endured the rejection of those who should have stood with you. This is how strength is formed."

"Cover me, Jesus," I cried.

I did not understand why He wanted me to remain there. I needed to get out.

Suddenly, I found myself pulling out of the water. I took hold of my horse and began walking along the shore. Night came quickly. I knew the Holy Spirit was still with me. I felt weak, but I kept moving.

Eventually, I climbed onto my horse, and Jesus appeared beside me.

"Keep riding," He said. "I am with you."

We returned to the fire, where George was waiting. Goldie looked exhausted.

"There you are," he said, smiling.

I looked at him, then reached for a towel. I asked Jesus why he was there. Jesus sat in a chair, our horses standing behind Him.

"George, these horses belong to Jesus and me. So even if Goldie is tired, you can't ride ours."

George moved behind me and climbed onto his horse.

"Let's go for a ride," Jesus said.

I was unhappy. I didn't want George there. I didn't want to face the feelings or the pain. I knew I wasn't what he wanted. I understood that. We were friends, but I was afraid I might want more and be hurt. I wanted it to be just Jesus and me. I wished he would go back down the beach and find someone else, someone more suited to him. Someone who was not me.

The ride was quiet and brief, and then we returned. George sat behind us in the shadows. I sat beside Jesus. Time passed, though I could not tell how much. It felt like minutes, but it could have been years.

I returned to the water, expecting the same peace I had felt before. The same beauty. The same joy.

But instead, I felt alone.

I saw creatures in pairs. Two shells are connected. The sun and the moon. Two stars. Two birds flying together. Two fish are moving side by side, their colors perfectly matched.

I could not ignore it anymore.

I did not want to be alone.

What could be done?

A porcupine cannot live with an eagle. A goat cannot run with horses.

I left the water and began walking along the beach, trying to move quietly so I would not be followed. I did not understand why George was there. I thought perhaps Jesus would speak with him and send him away.

Did Jesus not know that I was content with Him alone? Had I not shown Him that He was everything to me? That He was my love, my companion, my forever?

Why was this longing still there?

I walked for a long time. I did not want to return. But I grew tired and hungry.

When I came back, Jesus was cooking fish. He and George were talking as if they had always known each other. They welcomed me to sit with them.

I refused. I avoided their eyes and went back into the water.

Suddenly, I was pulled under.

There was no protection. No air. No way to breathe.

I slammed against a barrier beneath the surface, trapped behind it.

My late husband was there, but he did not help me. He did not see what was happening. He did not understand. He stood apart, unchanged, still caught in the same patterns he had lived in before. He was unaware of my need.

He was no longer in the water. He wandered along the shore, focused only on himself. He did not look back. He did not search for me.

Time felt frozen.

I could not move.

I thought I would die there.

I began to wonder if God was showing me my past again. If this was because I had chosen wrongly before. If I had lacked protection because I had not fully followed Him. Was this why I could not move forward?

Was this my consequence?

Was I meant to remain here?

Had I ruined everything?

I confessed again that I should never have married him. That I had disobeyed God. Was that why I walked alone now?

Was that why my words seemed to go unheard? Were You punishing me, Lord?

Maybe everything I have written is meant for another time. Maybe I am meant to remain unseen. Silent.

I had made a mess of everything. There was no way to fix it.

The weight of my books pressed against me as I sank deeper. Then Jesus came.

He pulled me out of the water and held my soaked books while I sat, catching my breath. Nearby, three horses stood quietly beside the fire.

As my books dried, Jesus and I strolled along the shore. We didn't talk much. I was too sad to talk.

When we returned, my books were dry and packed into a bag. The bag was heavy, and I had to carry it as I walked behind my husband.

He did not understand anything. He did not want to. He had lived so long numbing himself that he no longer saw clearly. Even when he tried to change, he returned to the same patterns.

I dragged the bag through the sand, moving farther from the water, farther from Jesus.

George sat in the chair, then left, then returned. I did not know what he was doing.

As I walked away, I saw George and Jesus sitting together by the fire.

I was walking alone.

But Jesus was still with me.

And finally, I understood.

George was there for what he had received from me and what he gave me on my journey on the paths. And now that my journey was ending, he was finished.

He was not there for me anymore.

And I will keep walking along the shore until I step into heaven with Jesus.

I am ready for a place where I am known. Where I am wanted. Where I am loved.

When I think of all the relationships I have had, I realize that my parents were the only ones who truly loved me.

They are the ones I think of as I walk.

I will keep walking until I cannot anymore.

And then I will go to them.

45

Troubled Slumber Path

I woke up in the cave with Jesus, alone. I felt deep disappointment because I was still on Earth. I hadn't eaten for seven days, and at that moment I realized I was being called to fast. The cave was cold and damp, and I sensed a heaviness of darkness even with Jesus beside me. My husband, still alive, was outside, looking up at the sky and laughing, unaware that I was only a few feet away with Jesus. I sensed darkness in him as he stared upward, uncomprehending. I wanted to run, but I had nowhere to go, and I couldn't run from my Lord.

George came to mind. I heard his voice accusing me, saying I was a terrible person, that I was letting the enemy into the camp, and that I would suffer for it for the rest of my life. He said I was defending what was clearly wrong, as if I were a lawyer arguing for guilt rather than the truth. I did not understand what he meant. I felt confused and alone.

"Jesus, what is happening? Why does it feel like I am being abandoned and forced to follow the man I married, who lived in darkness and is now gone? It feels like I am carrying the weight of that decision with me. I know I chose poorly when I entered that covenant, but what can I do now? I needed him, even though I knew he was not right for me. How else would I have survived? And why is George in my life at all? I am so confused."

"My dear, there is still much you need to understand. You need healing from what you went through. You trusted men for many years, but they could not save you. Only I can. When you chose your own way for a moment of relief, you opened a door that let the enemy trouble you. I allowed it, though it was not what I desired for you. You asked for a man, and you saw what happened when you pursued your own way instead of seeking Mine. Now you must learn to trust Me fully, as you have not before. You tried to fill the gaps with people and things that seemed right at the time, but they only covered your need for Me. Now those coverings have been removed. Trust Me completely. I will bring the right people into your life, those who are faithful and true. It is easy to say you will follow Me anywhere, but when that path requires you to walk alone, it becomes difficult. I know you desire protection and companionship, and you will have them in time. But some people cannot remain, and I will remove them when necessary. Remember, even I was betrayed by those close to Me. Each person chooses their own path. Judas chose to betray Me. Even those surrounded by light can still choose darkness. But I am always with you, guiding you in love."

"Yes, Lord, I see. But please help me understand. All my life, I have longed for love and a family of my own. Now I find myself without either, and it breaks my heart to think I may never have what I once hoped for. I feel alone. I know I shouldn't dwell on this because You are with me, but I am human. You created us to need one another. Sometimes it feels as if You did not fully understand what I needed in a man, even though You knew my deepest desires. Because I made so many wrong choices, I now carry the weight of this loneliness."

"Stay with Me. Remain in Me and let Me remain in you. In Me, you will find peace, contentment, and purpose. Be faithful where you are, here and now, in this place with Me. Do not see this as a place of isolation, but as a place of safety where I am strengthening you, making you less dependent on others. You have longed for Me, and I have been calling you. Now you are here. Rest. I am spirit, and I am with you wherever you are because you have welcomed Me. Stay present with Me. Leave tomorrow in My hands."

"Thank you, Jesus. I love you."

After this, I was troubled again. I slept and dreamed that George came to me and spoke with warmth, as if he cared deeply for me.

"That is not why I am here," he said, smiling in a way that unsettled me. "You are mistaken. What made you think I loved you? I have loved only once in my life, and I will not love again. It is not my fault that you lacked what you needed in your marriage, but you will not find it in me. I am sorry if you misunderstood anything I said. Look at yourself, then look at me. We are not suited for each other. I have been given a certain appearance, and you are plain. You have a good heart, but we will never be together."

I woke up crying, hearing a baby, though I could not find where it was coming from. I wondered if it was a child I had lost or one I would never know. I questioned why George's words affected me so deeply. I wondered if I had allowed something into my life that did not belong because of my longing to be loved.

Even with so many unanswered questions, I chose to obey what the Lord had asked of me. I fell asleep and dreamt I was in front of a fire in the white beach house. I was preaching, but when I woke up, I was alone with my cats in the cave. To release George, I prayed that he would find the woman meant for him, or that he would be removed if he was not meant to remain. I even imagined her name written in the stars, knowing that God names each one.

The last time I saw him, he was walking along the beach with his horse. I knew he would go on to find someone, and I would continue the path God had set for me. I would not stay behind, waiting. I did not need to see who she would be. I had spent too much of my life in the wrong relationships, and I did not want to dwell on what might have been if I had made different choices. I had often imagined myself to be more than I was, hoping for something that was never meant for me. I accepted that I had made my choices, and now I would live with them. I asked God to free me from the pain and to help me endure what remained.

Still, my heart ached. I thought of George often. We had shared so much, and I believed it was love. Perhaps I was wrong. But I understood now that it was part of a test, and I had to move forward.

During one of my walks, I saw a yellow butterfly moving alone in the sun, and then another joined it. I was grateful for that small sign. Whom have I in heaven but You, Lord, and on Earth I desire only You.

Winter was approaching, and the warm days were dwindling. I appreciated the small things. When the sun disappeared, the pain in my heart deepened. George had once been a light in those darker seasons. Now he was gone. I saw how easily I had been deceived. I accepted that whatever he was, I was not enough for him.

I found it hard to keep writing. Jesus still spoke, and I still listened, but there were days when I stayed wrapped in a blanket by the fire, waiting. It was quiet. Too quiet. He told me to wait and trust that this part was the hardest when I was separated from others. I was still human, and I felt the weight of it. I stopped believing my words would ever be heard widely. I would leave them behind when I was gone. I would also leave my children, who no longer came to see me or spoke to me. I did not understand why, but I accepted it as part of surrendering everything to Him.

I cried often. It was difficult to let go of the comforts of life and accept the absence of companionship I had always longed for.

I wondered if I would die in the cave. Only God knew. I could only see today. I told Him I was ready to go home, but He reminded me that the timing was His, not mine. If I were still here, there would still be purpose.

I often thought about the final days before George was no longer part of my life. He had become restless, like something trapped, pushing against every boundary until he finally broke free. I couldn't understand why he needed to leave so desperately. I was too much for him. I now refuse to believe that he loved me. That thought no longer holds. What remains is the understanding that I have often been the one left behind, the one overlooked, the one who was never chosen.

I overwhelmed him with my thoughts, my visions, my need for something deeper. To me, he was the most beautiful man I had ever known, and perhaps the only one I ever truly loved. Even so, I will carry that quietly.

I am weary of this world. The silence, the absence of family, the lack of connection, and the passing of days without meaning. I remember what it was like to be surrounded by voices and laughter, never imagining I would one day face the end alone.

Lord, I ask you, bring me home soon.

46

Muddy Path of Pain

It rained heavily yesterday, and I cried just as fiercely. The dark cloud within my heart felt endless, as if it would never clear. Today, a steady drip falls from the patch of still-green Earth above the cave entrance, echoing in my mind, loneliness, loneliness, loneliness. I remember speaking with conviction about my faith, saying I would walk alone if I had to, trusting my own resolve. But now that I am here, that resolve is weakening. It is painfully clear how naive I was to believe I could face everything on my own, how fragile my independence is when silence surrounds me, and every familiar voice is gone. I know John and Daniel were only part of a short season, and I will be with them again in eternity. That truth brings a quiet, confident smile.

It was cold and windy, and the sting of snow, instead of rain, made the weight of winter feel deeper and more real.

"Jesus, you forgot me."

"Faustina, turn around."

I turned and saw the child Jesus, with Mary and Joseph beside Him, and a great company of angels behind them. It felt like Christmas.

"I have not forgotten you. This is the moment I remembered you."

Then He told me to look up. When I did, the cave's roof lifted, and I saw countless angels worshiping the Lord.

"You were always Mine. You came into the world through your parents, but you belonged to Me before then. Every person born must decide whether to worship Me and walk in life or turn away and walk toward death. This is not a choice to be delayed, because that opportunity may not always be available. Whether they realize it or not, they are choosing even now as they walk their path. Many do not see where it leads or understand that it will one day end.

"I am shaping you and deepening your love for others. Family on Earth is temporary, but the soul is eternal. Relationships may change, yet I am giving you something permanent and unshakable amid your emptiness. Surrender to what I am doing in you, and let Me fill you.

"Why are you troubled by loneliness during the holidays? There would be no celebration without Me. Why isn't My presence enough for you? I have given you life, hope, resurrection, and eternity. You can choose gratitude whether you are surrounded by people or standing alone. You believe happiness depends on love staying around you in a certain way, but there is a deeper, lasting joy that I am guiding you into. There is a depth to My love you have not yet understood. Deny yourself, and you will see that I have filled you, and you will have more than enough to give.

"What you have seen on these paths is humanity choosing between the enemy and Me, who rules this present world. People will destroy one another when they remain apart from Me. The enemy hates those made in My image. He seeks power through destruction and pride, whispering lies into willing hearts so they harm others. People allow this influence into their thoughts, and it shows in their actions. The enemy promises power and freedom, but in the end, he brings destruction. Many walk this path, drawn by temporary pleasure and control. But it will not last. Humanity has been deceived from the beginning and will continue to be deceived until the end. Those who choose Me, even amid this, will receive an eternal reward.

"Time is limited. Every person must decide their eternal destiny. You enter this world with nothing and leave it the same way. In between, there is love, joy, sorrow, and the choices you make with the life I have given you. The end will come suddenly, and eternity will begin. Most people do not look beyond their time here, but those who do and choose Me will be granted a life that never ends. This life is a short testing ground, and the choices each person makes are very important.

"While you mourn your loneliness, George was traversing a fleeting path filled with temptation and confusion, leading him into the desert for a test of endurance. At first, he thought his task was to herd the cows to better pastures. Venomous snakes crawled out of their holes, and feral animals lurked in the shadows, ready to attack. As he and Goldie guided desert cattle toward a spot with fresher water and forage, she suddenly panicked and charged, crashing into a fence hidden by overgrown shrubs. Though severely wounded, she remained standing, shaken but alive. Exhausted by the ordeal, George had to rest.

"Gorgeous women of runway-model quality came to George as he slept deeply, his head resting on a stone, each alluring in her own way, as Satan tempted him to surrender to their charms. Some ladies had long, curly, dark hair and green eyes; others had piercing black eyes and short hair. One woman was everything he had ever dreamed of—stunning, tall, with soft blue eyes and flowing golden hair. She was one of a kind, molded by her many trials, or so she claimed. When she entered a room, all eyes were drawn to her. She spoke of Me as though she truly knew Me. In her seductive whisper, she cooed that George was the most handsome man she had ever seen and that God had brought them together. George, though definitely interested, slowly recognized this as a temptation, and his struggle to escape intensified. Suddenly, she began to grow—like an uncontrollable tree—seven feet, nine, twelve feet tall—until he realized that the Lord was stretching her so he could view her from a new perspective. What he came to see was eye-opening. Who was he trusting to fulfill his heart's desire, Me or himself? Was he fully waiting in faith for My perfect plan, or seeking to fill his heart with forbidden fruit while he waited, unknowing that the fruit was spoiling his taste for the good gift I was preparing for him?

"He woke with a new sense of My presence and vowed that even if he had to wait a lifetime, it would be worth it when it was My best."

47

The Final Call Path

The final drafting table turned completely white as the last souls arrived. Many people were running from the woman in black, choosing instead to come to Jesus. He was calling them into the light. But as soon as they stepped away, the tormentor appeared again, offering them other paths and promising they would be happier there. He claimed he could help them find their way again. The path to life was hidden, but it could still be found by those who sought Jesus with all their hearts.

Just beyond the gate, flowers were already beginning to bloom. Some people complained that the path was too difficult, too narrow. They longed for things to return to how they once were. They were not concerned about what was coming. There were rumors that the mark of the beast would soon be offered, yet they remained focused on Earthly desires. They wanted love, marriage, children, success, and comfort before that time came. Heaven felt distant to them, uncertain and unclear. They questioned which God was true, whether the God of Christians or the gods others followed. A thick fog began to settle, covering the paths. Soon, if they did not choose life, the choice would no longer be theirs. Many stepped back into the fog, and it closed around them quickly. Out of fear and attachment to the world, they chose darkness again, and in doing so, they could no longer see Jesus.

As I watched, a figure emerged from the shadows. A dark, threatening woman reached for me, trying to pull me away. I cried out for my children. I longed for home. I thought of my cats, of all I had lost. The woman mocked me. She told me to look at what my devotion had brought me. She urged me to focus on the life before me rather than on what I could not yet see. She questioned whether all paths did not lead to the same end, whether everything would not work out in the end as I once believed.

My feet felt heavy, as though I could not move. I reached toward the light, but I could not see it. Suddenly, I was back at the drafting table with John and Daniel. I asked what had happened, and they told me that the path to the kingdom comes through hardship. They reminded me that the enemy is real and that God's power is greater, and that I must resist what opposes Him.

Then I saw myself standing in a place of authority, speaking to those who held power. I could see their thoughts, dark and hardened. Some claimed to know Jesus. A few truly did. But most were driven by a desire for power and gain. I heard the Lord speak to me, telling me to speak what I saw in their hearts, to speak clearly, and then leave. I obeyed, though it frightened me. Some became angry at what I said, and at times, I ran from the room in fear. My heart felt heavy as I completed what I knew was my final assignment.

A path appeared before me. It looked dangerous, filled with shifting shadows and strange sounds. Thick bushes lined the way, concealing what might lie within. I did not want to go. I had not yet fully accepted suffering. Still, I stepped forward, my legs unsteady. The ground was rough and uneven, as though few had walked there. Small trees offered brief shade as the heat intensified. I hesitated, but something compelled me to continue. I questioned whether this narrow, difficult path could truly lead to life. It was so tight in places that I could barely move. It felt unsafe. I saw snakes, but they disappeared as quickly as they appeared.

"Jesus, I have only You. Please take my hand."

I moved forward slowly, each step heavier than the last. Then I saw footprints ahead of me, large and steady. When I stepped into them, I felt stable, though it was difficult to remain within them. I noticed things just beyond the path, beautiful and inviting. I could not tell whether they were blessings or temptations.

"Come and sit with Me for a while, Faustina. You are almost home."

The Lord took my hand. His hand was strong, marked by many scars. He gave me water and a small piece of bread. Even though I had very little, I felt renewed. I could now see clearly what was off the path. Bright packages of sweets, tempting and alluring. They promised pleasure but caused harm. They would create a craving that could never be satisfied. Still, I wanted them.

For a moment, I wanted to turn back—to return to the life I once knew. I longed for recognition and companionship. I missed chasing after what I never had. I no longer wanted to continue this path. I felt alone and questioned whether anything I had done mattered. I remembered that Jesus told me to write for eternity—that heaven sees and remembers. I believed that, but I still struggled. I wanted to leave the path, to forget what I was called to do—to live freely without restraint. But I knew I could not. I knew I was not home yet. The path continued day after day, and it felt endless. Fear pressed in from the darkness surrounding it.

"Jesus, give me strength. Help me not to fear what I cannot see. Strengthen me. If no one walks with me, will I still follow? If no one ever knows what I have done, will it matter? Will anyone remember me? Will my children remember me? I have always believed you could use me, but I do not feel that I have fulfilled that purpose. I remain hidden, though I sense something beginning to break through."

Jesus led me to the back of the cave. John and Daniel were gone. Eight angels sat around a table. They appeared small at first, but when they stood, they were immense, with wings stretching wide. I asked why they were there, but there was no answer.

Then Jesus spoke again, with sorrow in His voice. He said many are walking in darkness, even those who claim to know Him. They can no longer distinguish between light and darkness, and they no longer care. Those who truly belong to the light would recognize darkness and feel unsettled by it. But for many, it has become normal to shift between both, experiencing moments of light and then returning to darkness without conviction. Their hearts are becoming hardened.

He told me this path was the only one leading to true light. Many false lights exist, and many people believe the light resides within themselves. These individuals risk being led into darkness. Walking the path of true light is challenging; it entails hardships, sorrow, unanswered prayers, and loss. Darkness will inevitably arise, and forces will attempt to deceive and influence. It demands discipline, awareness, and a constant turning toward Him. However, those who remain committed will ultimately triumph. For a moment, I sensed Him depart and heard a loud crack, like a piece of pottery being stepped on. Out of the corner of my eye, I saw the most beautiful snake I had ever seen. Jesus swiftly stepped on its head, crushing it and pushing it aside. He then returned to my side.

He said many turn away because they abandon fellowship and believe that belief alone is enough. Yet knowing Him requires more than mere belief. It involves closeness, listening, and obedience. The path is visible to those who seek it, but those who drift toward temptation will become lost. People often leave this path because they grow disappointed, expecting life to be easier. But that is not the promise.

He told me to speak to those who are drifting, to warn them to open their eyes and choose the light while there is still time, because no one knows when their life will end.

48

The Path that Leads Home

I grew weaker each day, knowing it would not be long. The sand in the hourglass seemed to fall faster, unconcerned with the season's end. The thought of leaving this life filled me with quiet sorrow. Life had been hard, and my only true comfort was Jesus and His promise of new life. Because He lives, we will live also. Little by little, I sensed the final day approaching, a feeling that had followed me since childhood, when I was left alone at school or when my mother was ill, and I stayed home. I cried then as well, but this sorrow was deeper—a painful awareness of endings everyone must face. Even the Earth seemed to mourn, trembling under the certainty of change. It hurts. Our spirits may grow stronger, but our bodies grieve the dying. We shouldn't pretend it's easier than it is. Our bodies have held on to life through Earth's bounty, and our hearts have been sustained by love. This is what we have always known.

As my body began to give way, I drifted in and out of awareness. One moment I was with Jesus, and the next I felt the cold weight of the Earth and the heaviness of the blankets. It felt as though heaven were opening while Earth slowly released its hold. I thought I heard weeping, though I could not be sure. I had never felt deeply loved by anyone still living, so I did not expect anyone to grieve for me now. The scent of death lingered in the air, and time seemed to slow as it approached its end.

I had always known death was near. Even as a child, I thought about it often. How could anyone not think of death when it surrounds us? We are all moving toward it. The Earth itself is fading. To be born is to live, but it is also to begin dying, at least in the body. And yet we are given a choice: to face eternal death or eternal life. What a weight that carries. Many choose death because the small joys of this life feel too precious to let go. The invitation to follow Jesus, the only source of life, is often refused. Deception whispers that this present life is all there is, urging us to seek fulfillment now. Many give in to that voice and are led into sorrow and regret, choosing what fades over what endures.

With each quiet farewell, my soul felt the echo of loss. The child who never came home. Love that was never returned. Forgiveness that was never given. Opportunities that slipped away. Promises left unfulfilled. Each one felt like a small death, like another grave marked on a hillside where someone once lived. The sound of my mother's voice, the laughter of the family, all seemed distant, as if they had never existed. What remained felt like a storm that brought only destruction. Healing never arrived. Answers never came. Words left unspoken stayed that way. Each ending reminded me that my own was near, that my final breath would come soon.

As I surrendered fully to God at the end of this life, I reflected on everything that had weighed on me. The disappointments. The unanswered prayers. The loneliness. The rejection. The feeling of being forgotten, overlooked, never truly chosen. Soon, I would step into a different place, one where I would be known, wanted, and embraced. It would not feel like arriving somewhere new but like returning to where I had always belonged.

The wounds that would not heal, the heart that continued to ache, the closure that never came, all of it would be met with something greater. Praise would replace sorrow. What I had longed for would finally be fulfilled, not here but beyond this life.

I knew it was time to finish my story. The light of the Lord I had followed grew brighter even as my physical sight faded. I sensed the presence of many angels and saints, and I knew every step along the narrow path had been worth it. Even without earthly companionship, it had meaning. He was with me, and I was going home to a love I had not fully known, to kindness, compassion, and joy. I would not walk alone again.

The Earth darkened, and a new light began to emerge, one that would never fade. I moved toward it, finally free, my entire being filled with something new. I heard an angel choir as the very atmosphere changed, charged with life. I knew with certainty that even though I had walked alone, it had all been worthwhile. It will always be worthwhile. Deep within my soul, I knew beyond any doubt that I had never truly had to walk any path alone.

"Jesus, I'm home."

The End

About the Author

Lorene Masters is an accomplished poet and author of 12 books. Her books, such as *The Tin Trailer and Other Poems for the Hurting and the Hopeful*, *Chasing White Horses - Poetry for Women Who Love Too Much*, *The Women He Loved - Dramatic Monologues of Encounters with God*, and "*Hungry Heart - How One Woman Found Love*, have received critical acclaim. Notably, *Hungry Heart* won the Grand Prize Award of the Guideposts (Inspiring Voices) Book Publishing Contest, a testament to her literary talent.

When Roses Fall is not just a book; it's a call to action. It explores the serious issue of sex trafficking, challenging readers to be a part of the light that shines in the overwhelming darkness of this global problem.

Words in the Wilderness—Letters to My Bride offers short, encouraging devotions with Bible verses for meditation and prayer.

A Voice Was Seen—Visions of Eternity is a fascinating account of her journey into the spiritual realm. It encourages us that an incredible world awaits followers of Jesus.

The Cry of the Little Roses is for all who are waiting for the Lord to see and intervene on the world stage. It brings hope that he will rescue the littlest ones trapped in the horrors of sex trafficking and administer righteous judgment on the perpetrators.

Lorene, a radio personality for over 30 years and an actress, is also a survivor of eating disorders, a sex trafficking awareness advocate, and a Lyme Disease survivor. Her journey of resilience and determination demonstrates her strength and inspires many. She is known for her more than 40 original dramatic monologues about women transformed by the touch of Jesus.

www.ingramcontent.com/pod-product-compliance
Lightning Source LLC
LaVergne TN
LVHW010616100826
845148LV00014B/2990
* 9 7 8 1 7 3 7 3 8 6 1 7 9 *